How To Impregnate A "Pregnant" Virgin:

1.   Swallow the utterly scandalous rumor that your best friend's straitlaced younger sister is suddenly with child, even though she blushes at the mere suggestion of how babies are made!

2.   Even though it's definitely not *your* baby-on-the-way, offer to paint the little darling's room (pregnant women should not sniff paint fumes or climb ladders), escort her to the doctor (or drive during rush hour) and satisfy her late-night cravings (especially if what she craves is *you*).

3.   When your kisses explode into an undeniable need to consume and possess, sweep this woman into your steely arms…then into the bedroom.

4.   Brace yourself against the shock that the "pregnant" woman you just made love to was, until moments ago, a virgin!

5.   Apologize profusely for believing rampant rumors about her impending motherhood.

6.   Prepare to propose when you realize that you may have just turned the rumors of her pregnancy…to truth!

Dear Reader,

Thanks to all who have shared, in letters and at our Web site, eHarlequin.com, how much you love Silhouette Desire! One Web visitor told us, "When I was nineteen, this man broke my heart. So I picked up a Silhouette Desire and...lost myself in other people's happiness, sorrow, desire.... Guys came and went and the books kept entertaining me." It is so gratifying to know how our books have touched and even changed your lives—especially with Silhouette celebrating our 20th anniversary in 2000.

The incomparable Joan Hohl dreamed up October's MAN OF THE MONTH. *The Dakota Man* is used to getting his way until he meets his match in a feisty jilted bride. And Anne Marie Winston offers you a *Rancher's Proposition,* which is part of the highly sensual Desire promotion BODY & SOUL.

First Comes Love is another sexy love story by Elizabeth Bevarly. A virgin finds an unexpected champion when she is rumored to be pregnant. The latest installment of the sensational Desire miniseries FORTUNE'S CHILDREN: THE GROOMS is *Fortune's Secret Child* by Shawna Delacorte. Maureen Child's popular BACHELOR BATTALION continues with *Marooned with a Marine.* And Joan Elliott Pickart returns to Desire with *Baby: MacAllister-Made,* part of her wonderful miniseries THE BABY BET.

So take your own emotional journey through our six new powerful, passionate, provocative love stories from Silhouette Desire—and keep sending us those letters and e-mails, sharing your enthusiasm for our books!

Enjoy!

Joan Marlow Golan

Joan Marlow Golan
Senior Editor, Silhouette Desire

Please address questions and book requests to:
Silhouette Reader Service
U.S.: 3010 Walden Ave., P.O. Box 1325, Buffalo, NY 14269
Canadian: P.O. Box 609, Fort Erie, Ont. L2A 5X3

First Comes Love
ELIZABETH BEVARLY

Published by Silhouette Books
America's Publisher of Contemporary Romance

For Lori Foster and Jackie Floyd
and all the other members of
Ohio Valley Romance Writers
who got me "pregnant" at their conference.

And for Teresa Hill,
who made me write about it.

 SILHOUETTE BOOKS

ISBN 0-373-76323-9

FIRST COMES LOVE

This edition published by arrangement with Harlequin Books S.A.

® and TM are trademarks of Harlequin Books S.A., used under license.
Trademarks indicated with ® are registered in the United States Patent
and Trademark Office, the Canadian Trade Marks Office and in other
countries.

Visit Silhouette at www.eHarlequin.com

Printed in U.S.A.

Books by Elizabeth Bevarly

ELIZABETH BEVARLY

is an honors graduate of the University of Louisville and achieved her dream of writing full-time before she even turned thirty! At heart, she is also an avid voyager who once helped navigate a friend's thirty-five-foot sailboat across the Bermuda Triangle. Her dream is to one day have her own sailboat, a beautifully renovated older model forty-two-footer, and to enjoy the freedom and tranquillity seafaring can bring. Elizabeth likes to think she has a lot in common with the characters she creates, people who know love and life go hand in hand. And she's getting some firsthand experience with mother-hood, as well—she and her husband have a six-year-old son, Eli.

IT'S OUR 20th ANNIVERSARY!
We'll be celebrating all year,
Continuing with these fabulous titles,
On sale in October 2000.

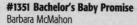
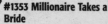

One

Tess Monahan never got sick. Never.

She had documented evidence of that in the attic of the house where she'd grown up in Marigold, Indiana—the house where she continued to live alone, now that her five older brothers were on their own and her parents had retired and moved to Florida. In her attic there were boxes and boxes full of school memorabilia, one of which contained thirteen certificates for perfect attendance, from kindergarten through twelfth grade.

She just never got sick. Never.

Even during the five years she had spent at Indiana University earning her bachelor's and master's degrees in education, she'd never missed a day of classes due to illness or anything else. Never. Even having taught first grade at Our Lady of Lourdes Elementary School for the last four years, she hadn't contracted so much as a sniffle to slow her down. Every single child in her class could come to school with some heinous virus, and Tess would remain hale and hearty. She just never got sick. Never.

Through every epidemic, big or small, that had hit her tiny hometown since her birth, she had remained perfectly healthy. She'd never had the chicken pox, never had the measles, never had the mumps, never had her tonsils out. She'd never run a fever. She'd never had allergies. She'd never coughed unless there was something stuck in her throat. She simply did not get sick. Ever.

Until today.

And today it was as if every single germ she had fought off in the past twenty-six years had come home to roost. With their entire bacterial families. But good.

She had awoken in the middle of the night feeling nauseated and it had only gotten worse as the wee hours of the morning wore on. She'd spent the last three hours hugging the commode, and now, as dawn crept over the horizon, she was certain she was going to die. And quite frankly, at this point—as far as Tess was concerned?— death would be a welcome diversion.

Unfortunately, death would have to wait. Because in a few short hours Tess was expected at the annual Our Lady of Lourdes teachers' appreciation brunch. She hadn't missed a single year, and this year would be no exception. Not just because she was adamant in meeting her obligations as an educator, but also because she would be receiving this year's Award for Excellence in Teaching. It was an honor she was proud to receive, and she wasn't about to disappoint her students, or her students' parents, or the rest of the Lourdes staff, by missing the presentation.

She would be there. She would accept the award graciously, with her heartfelt thanks. It was the least she could do to show her appreciation for her students' appreciation. Even if she did feel—and no doubt looked—like death warmed over as she extended those heartfelt thanks.

Tess groaned as she pushed herself up from the commode, then sighed as she leaned back to feel the cool tile wall through the white cotton tank she wore with her pajama bottoms. It must have been something she ate, she decided. After all, it was the middle of May, and the cold and flu season had long ago concluded. As she cupped her palm over her forehead and shoved her sweaty blond bangs out of her eyes, she realized she was burning up with fever. Whatever was assaulting her system, her body had called out every weapon it possessed to fight it. Maybe, with any luck at all, she'd feel better in a few hours.

Somehow she garnered the strength to turn on the shower, strip off her clothes and crawl under the tepid spray of water. Surely a shower, a dose of Alka-Seltzer and a few saltines would make a huge difference, she told herself. Surely the worst of her illness was over. Surely by the time she arrived at school, she'd be feeling good as new again. Surely she would live.

Surely.

Weakly, she rinsed her hair and shut off the water, then stepped out of the shower and toweled off. And although she really wasn't able to conjure much concern for her appearance, she wanted to look as nice as she could for the brunch and award presentation. Striving for comfort over anything else, she pulled a loose-fitting, pale-blue jumper over an equally loose-fitting, pale-yellow T-shirt. Then she dragged a comb through her damp, near-white, shoulder-length tresses and frowned at her reflection in the mirror. She didn't think she had the strength to lift a hair dryer for any length of time, so she tied her hair back with a blue ribbon and ruffled her bangs dry with her fingers as best she could.

Her fair complexion was even paler than usual, thanks to her sickness, so she donned a bit more makeup than she normally would. Unfortunately, she couldn't quite cover the purple smudges beneath her eyes, so she tried to be heartened by the fact that they made her eyes look even bluer somehow. Hey, she was known for making the best of every situation, wasn't she? Right now she'd take what she could get.

But even after completing her morning toilette, Tess continued to frown at the woman gazing back at her from the mirror. She looked like heck—as first-grade teachers at Catholic elementary schools were wont to say. There was no mistaking that she was gravely under the weather. She just hoped she could remain vertical long enough to accept her award.

Stumbling into the kitchen, Tess went immediately for the saltines, knowing she needed to put something in her stomach. She had some carbonated mineral water in the fridge, and she reached for a bottle of that, as well. Then she took a seat at the kitchen table and nibbled experimentally at her repast.

As she ate, she felt her forehead again and found that it was a bit cooler. The Alka-Seltzer must have helped some to bring down her temperature. Surprisingly, the crackers stayed down, too, and that helped some more. And the bottled water did seem to soothe her nausea to a considerable degree. Might not be a bad idea to take some with her to the brunch, though. Heaven knew she wouldn't be consuming any of the lovely dishes she knew would be served—fruit salad, blueberry scones, crepes, eggs Benedict….

Her stomach rolled again just thinking about it, and Tess reached weakly for the entire box of saltines. No sense taking any chances.

She filched a couple more bottles of fizzy water from the fridge, then stowed her booty in a nylon lunch bag decorated with the image of Disney's Cinderella—a gift from one of her students last Christmas. Then she tucked her bare feet into a pair of sandals, filled her oversize canvas carryall with her foodstuffs and all the necessary accoutrements of a first-grade teacher about to receive an award. Then, very gingerly, she headed for the front door.

She was just turning the knob when another wave of nausea uncoiled in her stomach. Oog, she thought. It was going to be a long—and icky—day.

Icky, however, didn't begin to describe the morning that unfolded after that. Tess did make it to school on time, but she had to head immediately to the girls' rest room once she got there. Worse than that, Sister Angelina, the school principal, caught her retching and encouraged her to go home and rest. Tess, however, had protested that she was feeling fine, and that her nausea was only temporary. And really, by the time she took her seat at the *Reserved* table beneath the speakers' podium set up in the cafeteria, she was actually starting to feel a little better.

The events following those, however, were much less welcomed, and much more nauseating—starting with the arrival at her table of Susan Gibbs. Susan was one of the other first-grade teachers at Lourdes, and since the beginning of the school year, she had thought...had assumed...had *expected*...to win the coveted Award for Excellence in Teaching. And ever since the announcement last month that Tess would instead be taking home that distinction this year, Susan had been a tad cool in her reception.

Of course, Susan Gibbs had also been Tess's rival since childhood for…oh, just about everything. Dark-haired, dark-eyed Susan had always been the perfect foil for fair Tess Monahan, as so many citizens of Marigold, Indiana, had pointed out over the years. So far, though, they were pretty well even, in wins and losses.

Tess had won the regional championship in the state-wide spelling bee in sixth grade, but Susan had won the regionals in the geography bee the same year. Tess had been the jay-vee football homecoming queen when they were freshmen, while Susan had been the jay-vee basketball homecoming queen. Tess had been the yearbook editor in tenth and eleventh grades, Susan the school newspaper editor those years. Tess had been Miss June on the school calendar when they were seniors, and Susan had been Miss October.

Of course, now Tess was about to receive the Award for Excellence in Teaching and Susan wasn't, but she didn't for a moment feel smug about that. She didn't. Not at all. Honest. It wouldn't be right.

"Good morning, Tess," Susan said as she folded herself into the chair next to Tess's.

"Hello, Susan," Tess replied as she shook a few saltines from the wax paper cylinder that held them. Then she pulled a bottle of carbonated water from her bag and twisted off the cap with a soft *psst*.

Susan noted her actions with a curious eye and frowned. "Gee, you look like heck this morning."

Tess threw her a watery smile. "Gosh, thanks, Susan. You always know the right thing to say."

"Sorry," the other woman said without a trace of apology. "But you do look like heck."

Tess just smiled a bit more waterily.

"By the way," Susan added, "I don't think I've congratulated you yet on winning the Award for Excellence this year."

Tess had started to lift the bottle of soda water to her mouth, but halted at Susan's comment. "No, you haven't," she said with a much less watery smile. Maybe Susan wasn't going to be as snotty as Tess had assumed.

But Susan said nothing more to expound on her statement—or to offer congratulations—so Tess lifted the bottle to her lips for a brief sip. She was about to compliment Susan on her springtime-fresh, flowered dress when one of the eighth-grade student volunteers came by with a coffeepot. As Tess sipped her water, Susan automatically turned her cup up and set it in its saucer in silent invitation for the girl to fill it. When the student had finished doing so, she turned to Tess, asking if she, too, would like coffee.

In response, Tess held up one hand, palm out, then placed the other over her still-rolling stomach. "Oh, no, thank you," she told the girl. "No one in my condition should be drinking coffee—trust me."

Susan fairly snapped to attention at Tess's comment. She dropped her gaze to the saltines and soda water sitting on the table before her, then to the hand Tess had placed over her stomach, then to Tess's face. Her mouth dropped open in shock, then an evil little smile uncurled on her lips.

"Tess," she said in a voice of utter discovery. "My gosh, you're *pregnant,* aren't you?"

The eighth-grader who had been pouring coffee had started to move away from the table, but at Susan's—loudly—offered assumption, the girl spun back around.

"You're gonna have a baby, Miss Monahan?" she cried—loudly. "That's so cool! When are you due?"

Before Tess had a chance to voice her objection, Susan replied in the voice of authority, "Well, if she's this sick now, I imagine she's only a month or two along. That would put delivery at...December or January. Oh, a Christmas baby!" she fairly shouted in delight. "How wonderful for you, Tess!"

Tess's eyes widened in complete shock. Try as she might to avert the charge, she was so stunned by it, that she had no idea what to say. Unfortunately, two women at the next table turned to gape at what they had just heard, and she realized she had *better* say something to avert the charge, before things went any further and got too far out of hand. For long moments, though, Tess could only shift her horrified gaze from Susan to the eighth-grader to the awestricken women at the next table, and back again. And for every moment that she didn't respond, Susan's smile grew more menacing.

"You *are* pregnant, aren't you?" she charged. "Tess Monahan, knocked up! And not married! Oh, I can't believe it! I can't believe you're *pregnant!*" Then a new—and evidently equally delightful—thought must have occurred to her, because her menacing smile grew positively malignant. "My gosh, who's the *father?* Your brothers are going to *kill* him!"

Only Susan Gibbs would ask such a forward, invasive question, Tess thought, the gravity of the charges being leveled against her still not quite registering in her brain. Finally, however, as she saw the two women at the neighboring table begin to chat animatedly with two others that joined them, Tess lifted both hands before her, palms out, as if in doing so, she might somehow ward off Susan's accusation.

"I am *not* pregnant," she assured both Susan and the eighth-grader who still stood gaping at her, coffeepot in hand. "It's the flu. I'm sure of it."

"Oh, please," Susan said indulgently, clearly not buying it. "It's May, Tess. Nobody gets the flu in May. Admit it. You're pregnant."

"Then it was something I ate yesterday," Tess said quickly. "Because I couldn't possibly be pregnant."

"You've never been sick a day in your life, Tess Monahan," Susan countered. "I remember the Fourth of July picnic when we all ate a batch of bad potato salad, and you were the only one who didn't get nauseated afterward. You have the constitution of a horse and a galvanized stomach to boot. *Nothing* has *ever* made you sick. Except, obviously, getting pregnant. Hey, I have three sisters with kids," she added parenthetically, "and I've seen how arbitrarily morning sickness hits. I can see it downing even you."

"It's *not* morning sickness," Tess insisted. "Because I'm *not* pregnant."

She may not know exactly what it was, making her feel this way, but she knew it wasn't...that. There was a specific activity in which one had to engage in order for...that...to happen, and Tess hadn't engaged in it lately. Or...*ever*. If she was pregnant, then she was about to receive a million dollars from the *National Enquirer* for the story surrounding her impending virgin birth. And she'd also be getting an audience with His Holiness Himself.

No worries there.

Susan, however, was clearly reluctant to disbelieve what she considered the obvious, because she continued, "Oh, come on, Tess. You don't have to be ashamed or embarrassed. It happens all the time these days. Even to good little Irish-Catholic girls like you.''

"Susan, I'm not—"

She turned, hoping to include the eighth-grader in her assurance, but to her dismay—nay, to her utter horror— the girl had wandered off to pour more coffee. Among other things. Even now Tess could see her chattering at Ellen Dumont, one of the math teachers, who immediately spun around in her chair to look at Tess with stark disbelief.

Oh, no, Tess thought. The girl might as well be broadcasting the news of her alleged pregnancy on CNN. Ellen was connected to everybody in town.

"Well, let me be the first to congratulate you," Susan said. "Many, many, *many* congratulations on your upcoming blessed event." Vaguely Tess noted that her rival was certainly capable of conjuring congratulations for a nonexistent pregnancy, if not for an actual award.

"Susan, don't. I'm not—"

But Susan only waved a hand airily in front of herself. "Oh, your secret is safe with me," she said. "I won't tell a soul."

Yeah, right. Like Tess was going to believe *that.*

"I just think it's so amazing," Susan continued with a slow shake of her head. "I mean, you're just so...straitlaced. So upright. So forthright. So do-right. So *boring,*" she added adamantly, in case Tess didn't fully grasp her meaning—as if. "I didn't even think you were dating anyone special," Susan added, "let alone having—"

"Susan," Tess quickly interjected. "I'm not. I'm not dating anyone special, nor am I...doing anything else with anyone special."

Susan gaped harder. "You mean it was *a one-night stand?*" she cried, even more loudly than before.

Now the women at the tables on *both* sides of Tess were gawking at her. And they were all looking at the saltines and sparkling water sitting on the table before her. Tess closed her eyes in mortification. Rumors in Marigold, Indiana, traveled faster than the speed of light. What was worse, though, the things piped over the Marigold grapevine almost *always* ended up being true. A little more embellished than usual, maybe, but still essentially true. If you heard it over the backyard fence in Marigold, Indiana, then, by golly, you could pretty much count on its reality, in one form or another.

By midafternoon, everyone in town was going to be certain Tess was pregnant. And they would be sure it had come about after some sordid one-night stand. She had to put a stop to this *now*.

"It wasn't a one-night stand," she said through gritted teeth.

"Then it *was* someone special," Susan surmised.

"No, it wasn't," Tess insisted. "It was nobody. I'm not pregnant."

But Susan was having none of it. When Tess opened her eyes, it was to see the other woman sitting back in her chair with a dreamy little speculative look in her eyes. "Let's see now, who could it be...?" she murmured. "Last time I saw you out with a man, it was at the Christmas bazaar. Donnie Reesor brought you."

"Donnie's just a friend," Tess said. "And you know it. And as everybody in town knows, he's about to ask Sandy Mackin to marry him."

Susan chuckled. "Well, this just might put a little crimp in *those* plans now, mightn't it?"

Tess closed her eyes again. "Susan, please..."

"Fine," the other woman relented. "Like I said, I won't tell a soul. I'll let you break the news to everyone when you're ready. 'Course, you won't be able to wait too long," she added jovially. "These things have a way of...showing themselves."

"There's no news to break and nothing to show," Tess said. "I—"

"Oh, but I can't wait to see how your brothers are going to respond to the news," Susan interrupted again. "Those Monahan boys were always ripe for a fight when we were growing up—anytime, anywhere. They're going to *pound* the father of your baby once they hear."

Although she was beginning to understand that the gesture was pointless, Tess tried one last time to deny Susan's assertion. "Susan, there is no father," she stated as levelly and forcefully as she could. "Because there is no baby. I'm sick, that's all. The flu, food poisoning, something. *Not* pregnancy, I assure you."

Susan leaned forward, wrinkled her nose in something akin to a smile and patted Tess's hand. "Don't you worry, Tess," she said. "Your secret is safe with me. Oh, look, there's Sister Mary Joseph. I absolutely *must* speak to her about a matter of *grave* importance."

And before Tess could stop her, Susan Gibbs rose from the table and scrambled across the room toward a gaggle of nuns. Tess buried her head in her hands and wanted to cry. The Award for Excellence in Teaching wasn't the only thing she would be up for today, she thought. No, by day's end everyone would be thinking of her in terms of Mother of the Year.

Two

The mood in the third bay of Will Darrow's Garage and Body Shop was, as always, laid-back. He had officially closed shop over an hour ago, at his usual weekday 6:00 p.m., and he relished the end of a productive day—a day of good, honest labor—like he relished nothing else in life. Cool jazz wafted from a portable CD player that sat atop the cluttered desk in the attached office, Will was sprawled beneath the chassis of a '68 Corvette that just so happened to belong to him, and his best friend, Finn Monahan, sat leaning back in the rickety desk chair he'd pushed into the bay, enjoying a long-neck bottle of beer.

Life, Will supposed, didn't get any better than this.

He had his own business—which was thriving nicely, thank you very much—and his best friend from childhood was his best friend in adulthood. Matter of fact, Will was still close to the whole Monahan clan, and although he hadn't thought it would be possible, he'd been drawn even closer into the circle of their affection since his father's death ten years ago. His old man had never remarried after his mother's death when Will was four, so the Darrow family had never numbered more than two. The Monahans, however, had always welcomed Will with open arms. They were the family he'd never had himself, right down to little Tess.

Of course, little Tess wasn't so little these days, which was something Will tried really, really hard not to notice whenever he saw her. Or whenever he thought about her. Or whenever he fantasized about—

Not that he *ever* fantasized about Tess, he quickly reminded himself. Not much, anyway. Well, hardly ever. Maybe just on those occasions when he saw her and tried really, really hard not to notice how she wasn't so little anymore. Unfortunately, with her looking the way she did now, it was pretty much impossible *not* to notice, because she was just so damned—

Best to think about something else, he told himself quickly as a vision of not-so-little Tess unwrapped itself in his mind. Because, as was frustratingly common nowadays, whenever visions of not-so-little Tess appeared in his brain, she was always not-so-little dressed. In fact, this particular image was one of her wearing a skimpy little scrap of pale-yellow lingerie and some of those fuzzy high-heeled things and—

Oh, boy. Not again.

Will squeezed his eyes shut tight and concentrated on other things—anything—that might make the vision of a scantily clad Tess Monahan go away. *The capital of Vermont is Montpelier,* he thought. *Babe Ruth hit 714 home runs in his career. The atomic weight of Boron is 10.81. A Scout is brave, trusty, kind, cheerful, obedient, thrifty, lusty…*

No, wait. That wasn't it. Where was he? Oh, yeah. Tess Monahan in wispy lingerie and—

No! That wasn't it, either.

Will sighed with much exasperation, reminded himself that Tess's oldest brother was in the room and started over again.

Marigold, Indiana, had been his home since he was seven and a half, and Finn Monahan had been his best friend since he was seven and a half and a day. Hell, Will could still remember when Mr. and Mrs. Monahan had brought Tess home from the hospital when he and Finn were ten, a tiny bundle of pink lingerie…uh, pink flannel…surrounded by five raucous little boys—six, if you counted Will. And Mr. and Mrs. Monahan always had.

Nope, Will thought as he twisted a wrench and loosened a lug nut—and recalled a faint image of Tess wearing that yellow lacy number—life definitely didn't get any better than this.

"Hello? Anybody home?"

Oh, great, Will thought. As if fantasizing—or, rather, *thinking*—about Tess Monahan wasn't enough to mess him up, now she had to come calling at the garage.

"Hey, Tessie!" he heard Finn call out from the corner of the room. "How was school today?"

How was school today? Will replayed the words in his head and smiled. He could almost erase ten or fifteen years from their lives and hear Finn asking Tess that very question as she bounded through the front door all scrawny legs and tattered braids. He settled the wrench onto the oily concrete and pushed himself out from beneath the 'Vette.

"Hi-ya, kid," he said as he rose, nearly choking on the last word when he got a look at Tess.

Kid. Right. With a body like hers and a mouth that

tempting, Tess Monahan was anything but. Even so, to remind himself just where he and she stood in the scheme of things, he strode over to where she had parked herself and, as had been his habit for two dozen years, ruffled her hair.

Bad mistake, he realized, as he invariably did upon completing the action. And not just because she turned a mutinous, murderous gaze on him for doing it, either. But because Tess's hair was like the finest silk, all soft and shimmery beneath his hand. He wondered how it would feel to, instead of rubbing her head like a good-luck charm, skim his palm lightly over those long tresses, or knife his fingers gently through the soft mass, or wrap a strand around his thumb and pull her closer, close enough to cover her mouth with his and—

Nothing, he told himself brutally. He would never do anything to—or with—Tess Monahan. She was a kid, even if she didn't look the part. And she was his best friend's sister.

And there was another reason, too, one Will didn't like to dwell upon, one that unfolded in his head, anyway, as he wiped his hands on his soiled coveralls. It was no secret to anybody in Marigold that Tess Monahan had always had a crush on him. Hell, Will had known it himself since she was ten years old. And as much as he thought about—all right, *fantasized* about—Tess, he would never take advantage of that crush. Because crushes had a way of turning into infatuation. And infatuation never led anywhere at all.

Yeah, Will knew Tess had a thing for him. And maybe, just maybe, he had a little bit of a thing for her, too. But that *thing,* for her, at least, was little more than a habit by now. If she had feelings for him, it was only because she'd had them for so long, they had become second nature to her. They weren't the result of an adult emotion that was destined for greatness. For Will to take advantage of her crush on him would be reprehensible, immoral. And it would only lead to trouble and a whole heap of hurt.

So Will kept his distance, because he knew it would be foolish to act on the attraction. Whatever might heat up between him and Tess would no doubt burn to a crisp in no time flat. Then the tenuous friendship they had would begin to feel awkward and uncomfortable. And in messing up things with Tess, Will might very well lose Finn, too. And Finn was the best pal he'd ever had.

"Hi, Will," Tess greeted him as she pushed her—soft, silky, shimmery—bangs back into place. And, as she always did when she saw him, she took a couple of steps backward.

He hated it that he intimidated her the way he clearly did. But hell, he had twelve inches and about eighty pounds on her—not to mention ten years—so there wasn't much he could do about it. And he knew she still felt embarrassed about that incident in her mother's kitchen four years ago, when she'd gone so far as to blurt out the reality of what a big crush she'd had on him all her life.

Truth be told, Will wasn't all that comfortable with the recollection of that, either. Even though there had always been a certain unspoken knowledge of her crush on him, neither of them had ever overstepped the bounds of propriety by actually talking about it. Not until the day Tess had just up and put voice to it the way she had.

But Will had moved on and forgotten all about the incident. He would put it right out of his mind. Totally and completely. Well, pretty much. Sort of. Hey, just because he couldn't quite bring himself to look Tess in the eye anymore, that wasn't any big deal, was it?

Nah.

"School was great today," she told her brother. But there was something in her voice that didn't quite ring true, something that sounded a little strained.

"They give you the big award?" Finn asked.

He'd risen from the chair long enough to give his sister a quick peck on the cheek, and now he folded himself back into it. The physical resemblance between the two siblings was amazing, Will noted, not for the first time. Except that Finn's hair was black instead of blond. Then again, all of the Monahan kids resembled each other— all had those piercing blue Monahan eyes, all were extraordinarily good-looking, and all of the boys, at least, were tall and fit and slim. Tess, too, was fit and slim, but at five foot two, she didn't exactly qualify for tall.

Upon closer inspection, though—but not *too* close— Will noted that she didn't exactly qualify for *fit* today, either. Even standing in a slash of evening sunlight that spilled through the open bay door, she seemed a little pale, a little fatigued. A little…sick? But that was impossible. Tess Monahan never got sick.

"It wasn't that big an award," she told her brother, scattering Will's thoughts. "But, yes, they gave it to me."

"Congrats again, Tess," Will said. And avoided her gaze.

"Thanks, Will," she replied softly. And avoided his, too.

A strange and uncomfortable silence followed, and for some reason Will got the impression that Tess wanted to say something, but wasn't sure how to go about it. Finn seemed to sense the odd mood, too, along with his sister's lack of color, because he tipped his head to the side to observe her.

"Everything okay, Tessie?" he asked in clear concern.

She nodded quickly. A little too quickly, Will thought. "Fine," she said, the word coming out clipped and fast. "Everything's fine. Perfectly fine. Why wouldn't it be fine? Do you know something I don't know that would cause it to be not fine?"

Will exchanged a hasty glance with Finn, then both men gazed curiously at Tess.

"Uh, no," Finn said. "I don't think so. You know more than me—you're the teacher, after all."

Tess seemed to relax a little but was still obviously guarded as she said, "So you haven't...you know... heard any...news?"

Will and Finn traded another one of those curious glances, then, "What kind of news?" Will asked.

Tess shrugged, but there wasn't anything casual about the gesture at all—it was as quick and anxious as the words that followed it. "I don't know," she said. "Just...news. Newsy...news. Something, you know... out of the ordinary. Something you wouldn't normally expect. Something that might shock or surprise you."

Will and Finn both shook their heads. "No," Will said. "It's been pretty quiet around here today."

Tess expelled a long, slow breath and swallowed with what Will could only liken to relief. Then, "Oh," she said quietly. "Okay."

"Is there something we should know, Tessie?" Finn asked, his voice laced with suspicion. "Something you want to tell us?"

"No!" she said, even more quickly than before. Immediately she blushed and dropped her gaze to the ground.

Oh, there was definitely something going on here, Will

thought. Tess was acting very strangely. She was usually the most cool, calm, composed person he knew. This wasn't like her at all.

"I mean," she began again, "uh...no. There's, um, there's nothing. And if you do hear any news," she added, glancing up, only to blush more furiously and drop her gaze again, "it's not true."

This time when Finn looked over at Will, it was with obvious apprehension. But all he said was, "Okay, Tessie. But if you want to talk about something..."

"Nothing," she stated emphatically. "I don't want to talk about anything. There is *nothing* to talk about."

"Okay, kid. Whatever you say."

"Will," she said, turning her attention away from her brother, "do you have that old tire you promised me for the kids in day camp?"

He nodded, putting aside—for now, at least—his concern over her strange behavior. "I found a truck tire," he told her as he went to retrieve it from out back. "It'll be a good size for the garden you want to make."

Within minutes he had the big tire loaded in her trunk for her, and Tess was climbing into her car and waving goodbye. Boy, she couldn't get out of there fast enough, he thought. He winced as she squealed her tires pulling out into the street.

"Man," Finn said when Will returned, "what's up with her?"

Will shook his head. "Got me. But there's something going on, that's for sure."

Finn sighed philosophically. "Well, whatever it is, it'll come out soon enough. Tessie never could keep a secret to save her life."

Will tipped his head toward the car he had been working on when Tess arrived. "Put on some coveralls and get under the car with me for a minute. I need your opinion on something.''

Within seconds—and without coveralls—Finn was rolling himself under the chassis from the side opposite Will, heedless of the dirt and grime that were already decorating his designer dress shirt and tie. Will shook his head in wonder at his friend's carelessness, but he figured Finn would just buy himself some new duds to replace the old ones, if they got dirty. And, hey, it wasn't like the guy couldn't afford it.

''What's up?'' he asked.

For long moments the two men pondered a complex mechanical dilemma, until the arrival of two red high heels—complete with shapely calves—appeared on the other side of the car.

A feminine voice called out, ''Hel-lo-o-o-o-o? Will, are you here?''

Yeesh! Abigail Torrance, Will thought. Probably with another casserole. Just what he needed. His freezer was already overflowing with Abigail's...creations. God, he hated casseroles.

''Go ahead,'' Finn said softly with a devilish smile, wresting the wrench from Will's fingers. ''I'll take care of this. I know how you feel about Abigail.''

Damn the man. The last thing Will needed was some woman underfoot. Still, Abigail—along with her trucking fleet—was one of his best clients, so he couldn't very well offend her by telling her to shove off, could he?

With a resigned sigh he pushed himself out from under the car and stood. Even though he knew it wouldn't do much good, he wiped his grease-stained hands on a grease-stained rag, then raked them both through his black hair. Akin to nothing, it occurred to him that he was long overdue for a haircut.

"Abigail," he said with a forced smile when he saw her. "What a surprise. And is that a casserole you're holding?"

She smiled in reply, turning her head in a purposeful way that Will knew was completed in order to show off the faint dimple in one cheek. She really was kind of pretty, he thought, and he had always preferred brunettes. But for some reason Abigail just didn't rev his motor— so to speak. Then again, few women did.

It wasn't that Will wasn't interested in the fairer sex— on the contrary, his...masculine drive...was probably a bit more, uh...more masculine...than that of a lot of men. But there were other things in life that took precedence. He just wasn't ready to settle down.

"You'll love it," Abigail told him coyly. "Tuna noodle surprise."

Will forced another smile. "Did I ever tell you that was my favorite? I love the surprise part. Not many women would think to include watermelon."

She batted her eyelashes. Actually batted them. Incredible. Then she purred, "Uh-huh. You did tell me it was your favorite."

"Wow," Will remarked dryly. "And you remembered. Imagine that."

She extended the large, rectangular container toward him. "Just heat it up at three hundred and seventy-five degrees for forty-five minutes, and it will be ready." She smiled again, more suggestively this time. "There's plenty there for two, you know."

Will nodded. "Great. You've got me covered for tonight and tomorrow night both. Thanks, Abigail. You're swell."

He tried not to choke on that last part, and hoped his dubious gratitude was convincing. He must have been at least marginally successful, because although she pouted at his rejection of her more-than-obvious offer, she quickly recovered and smiled again.

"Have you heard the latest news?" she asked.

Oh, boy. Gossip. Gee, Will just lived for that. "Um, no, Abigail, can't say that I have." He turned quickly toward the office with the pretext of taking the casserole in there, hoping the sight of his back would let her know just how anxious he was to hear whatever choice item she might have—namely, not anxious at all.

But Abigail, as usual, didn't take the hint. "It's about Tess Monahan," she said, nearly breathless with excitement.

Will spun around, his gaze inevitably drawn to the trouser-clad legs sticking out from beneath the 'Vette. The trouser-clad legs that belonged to Tess Monahan's oldest brother. The trouser-clad legs that Abigail obviously hadn't seen.

"Uh, Abigail?" Will began, hoping to cut her off.

Although he didn't for a moment think there could be anything shocking or controversial about Tess—hey, after all, it was *Tess*—he didn't think it prudent for Abigail to be gossiping about her in front of one of her brothers. It just wasn't polite. And Finn, like all of his brothers, had just a bit of a quick temper, not to mention a protective streak a mile wide, when it came to his kid sister. None of the Monahan boys would much appreciate Tess's being talked about. Even if the talk was harmless. Which Will was sure this would be.

Because, hey, after all...it was *Tess*.

He opened his mouth to announce Finn's presence, but Abigail, evidently much too excited to be put off any longer, blurted out her big news before he had the chance. And boy, oh, boy, what news it was.

"Tess Monahan has been knocked up!" she cried almost gleefully.

"What?!"

Will was surprised to discover that the outraged exclamation erupted not from the man beneath the 'Vette, but from his own mouth. And as if that weren't bad enough, to punctuate his utter and complete shock, he dropped the casserole—tuna, noodle *and* surprise—onto the cement floor with a resounding crash.

Abigail, too, was taken aback by his response—literally. She took one giant step backward, as if she feared Will was going to bolt right over her on his way to—

To do what? he wondered. Right this egregious wrong? Beat the hell out of whoever was responsible for Tess's condition? Break the jaw of whoever had started this stupid rumor in the first place? Even if it were true, what the hell business was it of his if Tess Monahan had gotten herself—

Knocked up?

Tess?

No way.

He spared a quick glance at Finn's legs, which were still sticking out from under the car and, surprisingly, weren't quivering with rage. Either he hadn't heard Abigail's announcement—which Will found *highly* unlikely—or else he was waiting to hear the rest…before he went out and thrashed the son of a bitch responsible for Tess's predicament.

"No way," Will said, turning back to the messenger, voicing his thoughts out loud. Though whether that was for Finn's benefit, for Tess's benefit or for his own benefit, he honestly wasn't sure. "You must have gotten your wires crossed somewhere, Abigail. Tess Monahan isn't that kind of girl."

In response Abigail chuckled, and Will couldn't help but think that there was something almost triumphant in the sound. "She is now," Abigail said. "I saw her myself this morning at the teachers' brunch. She was sick as a dog."

Will shook his head in denial. "Tess has never been sick a day in her life."

"I know. That's what *I* said. The only thing that could make her this sick is morning sickness. Sister Angelina saw her barfing in the girls' rest room, too."

Will shrugged it off. "Oh, big deal. So Tess has the flu." But even he had trouble believing it. "That doesn't mean she's pregnant."

"There's more," Abigail said.

Yeah, Will would just bet there was. "Like what?"

Abigail took a few steps closer—carefully avoiding the spilled casserole—as if wanting to pull him physically into her conspiracy. "Well, for instance, about two months ago, Dolores Snarker was up in Bloomington, and she saw Tess at a Motel Six."

Will somehow refrained from rolling his eyes. "So? A lot of people stay at motels, Abigail. And believe it or not, most of them don't get pregnant."

"Yeah, but Dolores saw Tess go into her room one night with a *man*."

This Will found hard to believe. He also found it hard to digest, because his stomach pitched at hearing the revelation. But even if it was true that Tess had been with a man—*Oh, God*—it didn't mean she was pregnant. It made him feel a little sick—all right, it made him feel a *lot* sick—but it didn't mean Tess was pregnant. Probably. Then again, she *was* pretty naive, he reminded himself. She might not take the proper precautions if she found herself in that kind of situation. She was so trusting.

"That's not proof of anything, Abigail," he said, in spite of his misgivings.

But Abigail ignored his objection. "*And,*" she continued, "my aunt who works for Dr. Schwartz, the OB-GYN? She said Tess had an appointment last month."

Will felt himself blushing at the mention of a...of a...of one of those...doctors...but, again, it wasn't conclusive proof of anything. "It's my understanding," he said, "that women go see the...the..." He growled under his breath. "That women have appointments like that every year."

"Ah, but it was Tess's second visit in two months," Abigail told him.

"Yeah, but still..." Will objected. Though not quite as strenuously as before.

"*And,*" Abigail continued happily, "Tess was in Bonnie's Baby Boutique a couple of weeks ago, and Bonnie herself said Tess bought almost a hundred dollars worth of baby clothes and stuff."

"It was probably a gift," Will pointed out, though it was unlikely. Nobody in Marigold who was close to Tess was pregnant.

"That's some gift," Abigail replied dubiously.

"Tess is a generous person," Will countered.

But his objections now were halfhearted, at best. There sure did seem to be an awful lot of evidence against Tess. And although gossiping was a pretty stable pastime in Marigold, hardly anyone could dispute that what went around almost always turned out to be true. Marigoldians might be rumormongers, but they were generally pretty good about keeping their facts straight. Even Will, who avoided the rumor mill, knew that.

Abigail stepped back again. "Well, nuns don't lie," she said, "and I heard about Tess's condition from both

Sister Mary Joseph and Sister Margarite. She's pregnant, Will. And all of us are just dying to know who the father is. Susan Gibbs said she heard Tess say herself that it was a one-night stand.''

"*What?*"

Again, much to Will's dismay, the outcry came not from under the 'Vette, but from the depths of his own dismay. Tess Monahan pregnant. And by some jerk who'd loved her and left her in one night. He could scarcely believe it.

But rumor, at least in Marigold, Indiana, didn't lie. Tess Monahan was going to have a baby. And Will Darrow had no idea what to do.

Three

By week's end, after three days of suffering from the flu, Tess was feeling a bit better. Although she was still weak and her appetite hadn't returned to full capacity, her stomach was no longer rolling, and her fever had eased. Even so, she had readied herself for an early bedtime tonight, just as she had for the three evenings prior, and had already changed into her nightclothes—a powder-blue T-shirt and a fresh pair of pajama bottoms, these patterned with puffy white clouds. And she had just retired to the couch with a new book that a number of first-grade teachers on the Internet were touting as a wonderful educational aide—*Raising a Creative Child in Modern Times*—when the doorbell rang.

Tess sighed with heartfelt exasperation at the intrusion, then settled the book, spine up, on the sofa cushion beside her. Honestly. After the three days she'd just survived, the last thing she wanted or needed now was a visitor.

Having done her best this week to fend off—with not particularly effective success—all the speculation and congratulations about the birth of her upcoming, though nonexistent, baby, she was ready to scream at the next person who brought it up.

Marigold being the kind of place that it was, there probably wasn't a soul around who hadn't heard about— and been convinced of—her ''condition'' by now. Her visitor this evening, she was certain, was yet another Marigoldian who had come to either speculate or congratulate.

Or, worse, to offer *help*.

Carol McCoy, up the block, who had four teenagers, had met Tess at the front door when she'd arrived home from school that first day of the rumors, and the other woman had been pulling a wagon loaded with three big boxes of hand-me-downs. They were her children's cast-offs that Carol had been storing in the basement, knowing that someday they'd come in handy for some expectant mother.

Tess had tried to talk Carol out of her donation, had assured her that there must be someone out there who was more deserving—someone who was oh, say... pregnant, for instance, *un*like Tess—but Carol would have none of it. She'd assured Tess that she wouldn't tell a soul about her condition, that she'd take the secret to her grave—which, of course, wouldn't be necessary, because it wouldn't be long before *every*one in Marigold knew, would it?—and had hustled back down the street to meet her own brood.

Tess had actually followed her neighbor halfway down the block, assuring Carol all the way that there would *be* no baby, because there *was* no condition, because she *wasn't* pregnant, but Carol had only nodded indulgently, murmured "Of course, of course" a few times, and told Tess to keep the clothes, anyway, *just in case*. So now the boxes were stacked haphazardly in Tess's living room, and she had no idea what to do with them.

Nor did she know what to do with the boxes of maternity clothes stacked beside them that Rhonda Pearson and Denise Lowenstein had donated to the cause. Nor did she know what to do with the big bag of infant toys Cory Madison had brought over. Nor the crib that Dave and Sandy Kleinert had given her—the one that was still sitting in pieces, propped against the wall, where the couple had left it until Dave knew which room would be the nursery, after which, he'd promised Tess, he would come back over and reassemble it. And just that afternoon, Mr. Johanssen, whose backyard abutted Tess's, had brought over a beautiful handcrafted cradle.

No matter how often—or how hard—Tess had objected to the gifts, her neighbors had only smiled and told her to keep them, *just in case*.

Whoever was at the front door now would be no different, Tess was sure. Because in spite of her adamant denial of the rumors of her pregnancy, nobody—but *nobody*—had believed her. The Marigold grapevine was an omnipotent power, infinitely more persuasive than little ol' Tess Monahan could ever hope to be. If rumor had it that she was pregnant, then according to Marigold canon, she *was*.

Instinctively she dropped a hand to her belly as she went to answer the front door, as if she herself almost believed she was nurturing a new life there. Boy, small-town gossip sure could be convincing, she thought as she tugged open the door.

And, boy, it sure could be humiliating, too, she thought further when she saw who stood on the other side.

Because she could think of no reason on earth why Will Darrow would come calling at her house, unless it was because he had finally heard talk about her imaginary pregnancy. And realizing that Will must be thinking it was true—why else would he have come over?—Tess felt the heat of a blush creep from her breasts up to her face. Then again, she always blushed when she saw Will—or even thought about him, for that matter—so why should this episode be any different?

Maybe, she thought, it was different now because deep down she'd always hoped that someday she *would* get pregnant and that when she did, Will Darrow would be the father of her child. That would of course be—at least in her fantasy—because he was her husband, too. And *that* would of course be—likewise at least in her fantasy—because he had fallen head over heels in love with her.

Hey, it was *her* fantasy. She could make it as outrageous as she wanted to. And having Will Darrow fall in love with her? Well, things didn't get much more outrageous than that. He still ruffled her hair whenever her saw her. Ruffled. Her. Hair. Oh, yeah. That was *always* a precursor to romantic love. To Will, obviously, she would always be ten years old.

Involuntarily—and hopefully surreptitiously—Tess scanned her visitor from head to toe. She couldn't help herself—she didn't get that many chances to scan him up close this way. Even though he had been her oldest brother's best friend since childhood, these days, she saw very little of Will. One might have thought—might have hoped—that seeing so little of him would cause her childhood crush on the guy to finally go away. Instead, that old saw about absence making the heart grow fonder had

come way too true. Because Tess's heart—among other
body parts—was *very* fond of Will Darrow.

Always had been.

Always would be.

Then another thought struck Tess. If Will had heard
about her "condition," then Finn had probably heard by
now, too. And if Finn had heard...

Oh, boy.

She didn't even want to think about the rampage that
must be going on down at Slater Dugan's Irish Pub. No
wonder Will was at her front door. He was probably
looking for bail money.

At thirty-six years old, Finn Monahan was a fine, up-
standing citizen and a bastion of the community, a complete 180-degree version of the quintessential bad boy
he'd been in his youth. Until someone threatened or bad-
mouthed a member of his family. Or, even more unfor-
givable, said a cross word about Violet Demarest, who
didn't even live in Marigold anymore, not since she'd
married and moved away, but whom Finn had elevated
to a pedestal—nay, an *altar*—a lo-o-o-o-ong time ago.

But whenever one of those two things happened, then
Finn Monahan could be counted on to revert right back
to the surly adolescent of two decades ago, the one who
was always ripe for a fight. There was no question that
talk of his little sister getting knocked up would put Finn
in a rare—and very bad—humor.

"Is he in jail again?" Tess blurted out before she could
stop herself.

It made for a less-than-welcoming greeting, she knew,
but that was the first thought that went through her head
when she saw Will. Oh, all right, the *second* thought that
went through her head when she saw him. The first

thought had been what it always was—that he looked really, really yummy.

His blue eyes were complemented by a blue chambray work shirt that was nearly the same color, and by blue jeans that were lovingly faded and torn at one knee. His overly long, black hair had been ruffled by the late-evening breeze, and the swiftly setting sun lit silver and orange fires ablaze amid the highlights. A day's growth of dark beard shadowed the lower half of his face and throat. Anyone else might find him menacing or intimidating. Tess just found him adorable.

But the last time she'd seen Will alone at her front door this way, it was because he'd come to tell her that Finn had been arrested for throwing a chair through the front window at Slater Dugan's Irish Pub. That actually would have been one of Finn's lesser offenses, if it hadn't been for the fact that Dennis Matheny had been sitting in the chair when it went through the window. But Dennis had asked for it—he'd called Violet Demarest the Whore of Babylon, right to Finn's face. Hey, Dennis was lucky Finn hadn't fulfilled his childhood fantasy of becoming an astronaut by sending him straight into orbit.

At hearing Tess's question, Will, who had been looking very uncomfortable when she'd opened the door, now looked very confused. Well, he still looked very uncomfortable—which was pretty much how he always looked whenever he saw Tess, doubtless because he knew what a raging crush she'd had on him since she was ten years old—but he looked confused, too.

"Is who in jail?" he asked.

"Finn," she clarified. She still couldn't shake the notion that her big brother had done something stupid in response to very real allegations about her very nonexistent pregnancy. "What's he done?" she asked further.

"He hasn't hurt anybody, has he? Dugan's Pub is still standing, isn't it?"

Will narrowed his eyes in even deeper confusion. "Finn's fine," he said. "I mean, I guess he is. He was fine when I saw him this afternoon. Pretty much," he qualified mysteriously.

In spite of the mystery, Tess breathed a sigh of relief. Good. Maybe Finn hadn't heard, after all. Actually, come to think about it, none of her brothers seemed to have heard about her rumored condition, because none of them had contacted her. Of course, Sean was out of town, and Rory was in deep research mode these days. Connor would just naturally ignore anything he heard through the grapevine, but Cullen usually bought in to talk. And Finn...

Well, Finn always knew what was going on in Marigold. So if Finn hadn't heard, then maybe things weren't as bad as Tess thought. And if Finn hadn't heard, then Will probably hadn't, either, in which case she was worrying for nothing. Except for the fact that the man she'd had a raging crush on since she was ten years old was at her front door, and she was standing there in her jammies, yammering incoherently at him.

Oh, but hey, other than *that*...

"Um, then...what are you doing here?" she asked him.

He went back to looking merely uncomfortable and didn't meet her gaze. But then that was hardly surprising. Will Darrow hadn't met her gaze squarely since...

Well, Tess couldn't really remember the last time he'd met her gaze squarely. Certainly not in the four years that had passed since she'd returned to Marigold after graduating with her master's in education from Indiana University. Her mother and father had thrown her a graduation party the month before they'd moved down to Florida, and Will, of course, had attended. At one point Tess and Will had ended up alone in the kitchen of this very house, and she—after having a little too much of her mother's infamous Pink Parisian Punch—had breathlessly blurted out something about how she'd always had *such* a raging crush on Will.

She had been mortified after doing it, of course, but she'd figured Will would just laugh off the comment and go back to the party and totally forget about it in five minutes' time, because he'd *never* taken her seriously. But Will hadn't done any of those things.

Except, evidently, take her seriously.

Because, much to her amazement, he'd blushed like a schoolboy, had stammered something unintelligible and had bolted for the back door. He'd fled the party completely and hadn't returned, and ever since then he hadn't been able to be around Tess without seeming—without *being*—extremely uneasy.

Me and my big mouth, she thought now, not for the first time. Had it not been for her imprudent revelation about the raging crush thing, she might still be able to harbor it in secret, and Will would be less hesitant to be around her. As it was, whenever they had family gatherings—and family gatherings always naturally included Will—he managed to stay in one room while she was in another. Or, if they were forced to be in the same room, he made it a point to keep them on opposite sides at all times. Tess was almost never close enough to him to actually touch him.

But she was now.

Because now he stood just over the threshold, scarcely two feet away. Now, had she a mind to, she could reach right out—and up—to cup his cheek with her palm. Now, had she a mind to, she could push herself to tiptoe and brush her lips over his. Now, had she a mind to, she could hurl herself shamelessly into his arms and wrestle him to the ground and have her way with him.

But of course, she'd *never* have a mind to do that. Not while he was in the immediate vicinity, at any rate.

"I'm here," he said, reminding her that she had asked him a question that required an answer, "because I promised your brother I'd come over and talk to you."

"Why doesn't he come over and talk to me himself?" she asked, thinking it a very good question. Unless...

Will closed his eyes briefly, then opened them again, and, as always, Tess marveled at how blue they were. "He was afraid if he came over to talk to you himself, he wouldn't do any talking. He'd just do a lot of exploding."

Uh-oh. That didn't sound good. That sounded like... "He's heard about my condition, huh?"

Will went a little gray at the question. "Yeah. He's heard about you being pregnant."

It took Tess a moment to realize how badly she had misspoken, then, "No!" she shouted, more loudly than she had intended. "That's not what I meant. I'm *not* pregnant."

Will gaped at her. "Tess, you just admitted it. And everybody knows about it, so you might as well stop denying it."

She shook her head vehemently. "I did not admit it. I just misspoke. I'm not pregnant. I'm not."

Will, however, didn't look anywhere near convinced. Then again, why should he? she thought. The Marigold grapevine had spoken. The announcement might as well have been engraved on stone tablets and presented by a burning bush.

"Tess, you don't have to keep denying it. Nobody thinks any worse of you," he told her. "Everybody just wants to help. That's why I'm here, too."

"You're here to keep my brother from sending my couch through my living room window," she corrected him.

He shrugged conspicuously. "Yeah, well...that, too."

"It's not true, Will," she said, even though she could see quite plainly that the denial would be pointless. "I'm not pregnant. I've had the flu. I would never... I couldn't possibly... There's no way I'd..." She gave up when she realized she wasn't finishing a single thought.

Will, however, continued to gaze at her with what she could only liken to pity. "Finn knows, too," he said again, unnecessarily. "He was in a state the other day, when he found out, let me tell you. I managed to convince him to give it a few days before he spoke to you, to cool off. Then I convinced him to let me come over and do the talking instead."

"Why?" she asked warily.

"Because he hasn't cooled off," Will said simply. "Sean still doesn't know, because he's still in Indianapolis, and I don't think Rory's heard, because he's been holed up at the library all week, and you know how he gets when he's in Deep Thought—he doesn't hear anything *any*body says. But Connor and Cullen are looking to kick some butt. It's not an easy thing, keeping your brothers at bay, Tess. They made me promise to report back as soon as I talk to you. But they realize they can't be reasonable about this right now. So they're letting me mediate."

"Even Connor believes it?" Tess asked incredulously. "But he never believes anything he hears on the grapevine. He's the last great skeptic."

"Hey, the evidence speaks for itself."

Evidence? Tess wondered. What evidence? Just what was everyone saying about her behind her back?

"I've had the flu, Will," she insisted. "That's all there is to it."

Will inhaled a deep breath and released it slowly, but he still didn't look convinced of her...nonmaternity. What he did look, she thought, was, well...really, really yummy.

"You've had the flu," he echoed dubiously.

She nodded.

He hesitated a telling moment before pointing out, "You've never been sick a day in your life. You'll forgive me if I—along with everyone else in Marigold—have a little trouble believing that you suddenly contracted the flu. Especially since it isn't even the time of year for it. Nobody else in town has the flu, Tess. Just you. Kinda suspicious, I say."

"Then it was something I ate," she insisted. She told herself she didn't have to defend herself—to Will or anyone else. Despite that, she felt obligated to do so just the same.

"Tess, you have the stomach of an ox," he pointed out.

And, oh, wasn't *that* just the thing a woman wanted to hear from the man for whom she'd been carrying a torch for more than a dozen years. "An ox," she echoed flatly.

He had the decency to look apologetic, even if he didn't apologize per se. "You know what I meant. You're a woman who can eat jalapeños straight from the jar without batting an eye. Though I wouldn't recommend it now. Not in your condi—"

"Oh, Will," she moaned. "Not you, too. Don't tell me *you* believe it."

"Well, what else am I supposed to believe?" he demanded, sounding as upset about the development as she was. "*Every*body's saying you're pregnant. Even nuns, Tess. Who can argue with nuns?"

But all she could offer in response was another disappointed, "Oh, Will."

He might not *want* to believe she was pregnant, but he did. Tess sighed fitfully and ran a restless hand through her bangs. Then, resigned to her fate, she tugged the door inward and stepped aside.

"You might as well come in," she said. "I have a feeling it's going to take a while to explain things to you and change your mind. Then you can report back to Finn and the boys after we've talked."

Will was obviously hesitant about entering, though. Which was odd, because he'd probably been inside the Monahan house more times than he'd been in his own when he was a boy. There had been so many nights when Will and Finn had played so late, or studied so late, or talked so late, that Will just naturally spent the night. And although she would never, *ever,* confess such a thing to *any*body, there had been nights when Tess had sneaked into the bedroom Finn shared with her second-oldest brother, Sean, just to watch Will Darrow sleep.

Now, as he cautiously crossed the threshold and entered the house, Tess couldn't help recalling those nights, couldn't help remembering how a younger Will had looked, sleeping shirtless and restless in a slice of silver moonlight.

He'd been slim, but solid, as a youth. As a man, he was still solid—*way* solid—but he had filled out, too. A lot. As he squeezed past Tess—careful not to let any part of his body come into contact with any part of hers—he towered over her by nearly a foot. He was twice as broad as she was, too, though that wasn't really saying much. Tess had one of those fast metabolisms that left her looking far too willowy for her liking—or would have left her looking willowy, anyway, had she been taller than five foot two. As it was, to her way of thinking, she just looked scrawny.

"Abigail Torrance stopped by the garage the other night," Will began without preamble as Tess closed the door behind him.

"Gee, what else is new?" she asked as she motioned him into the living room. She told herself she did *not* sound petulant as she continued, "Abigail stops by the garage just about every night. What succulent little morsel did she bring you to eat that night?" *Besides Abigail Torrance,* she then added uncharitably to herself.

"That's not important," Will said as he strode toward the sofa. "What *is* important is—"

He halted midstride and midsentence, his gaze fixed on the book that was lying faceup on the sofa cushion— the book titled *How to Raise a Creative Child in Modern Times.*

Oh, great, Tess thought. She knew exactly what he was thinking, so before he had a chance to say anything, she hastily explained, "It's for school."

"You're reading how-to-raise-a-kid books for school?" he asked dubiously.

She nodded. "How-to-raise-a-kid books make great educational aides. A lot of teachers are reading that book. Teachers who *aren't* pregnant," she added pointedly.

Will clearly wasn't swayed in his opinion. He hooked his hands on his hips—Tess tried not to drool at the way his shirt gaped open a bit over the dark hair beneath— and just got right to the matter at hand. "Talk has it that you were seen at a motel a while back with a man."

Now this was news to Tess. And it frankly surprised her that the Marigold grapevine—enthusiastic though it might be—would perpetuate something so unfounded and malicious. Not that passing along the false notion that she was pregnant was particularly kind, but it had at least been grounded in some kind of odd reality—the impression that she had been suffering from morning sickness and had herself made a reference to her ''condition.''

Her being with a man at a motel, well... That was just plain not true. And it wasn't normal for the local gossip to be *that* inaccurate. Although Tess *had* stayed at a motel a couple of months ago, she had done so alone. She couldn't imagine why anyone would think she'd had company.

''Up in Bloomington,'' Will said, clearly detecting her confusion.

''Yeah, I know,'' she replied. ''I did stay at a motel up there while I was attending a week-long teachers' conference in March. But I was always alone in my room.'' Then a memory erupted in her brain. ''Oh, except for that one guy that one night,'' she amended. ''But that was nothing.''

Will's cheeks went ruddy at her declaration, his anger evident in the rigid stance of his entire body. ''So then it really was a one-night stand that left you pregnant.''

It took a moment for the comment to register in Tess's brain, so bizarre was it. But when it finally did register, ''*What?*'' she asked, incredulous.

Will blew out an exasperated breath and shoved both hands brutally through his hair. ''Susan Gibbs said you told her that the baby's father was a one-night stand. I was sure she was making it up, but hearing you—''

''Will!'' she exclaimed, stung that he could believe

such a thing, even reluctantly. "I did *not* have a one-night stand!" Good heavens, she could see Susan wanting to believe the worst in her, but Will? He might as well have slapped her, so profound was the feeling of betrayal that knifed through her.

He was visibly relieved by the declaration. Not a lot. But some. Unfortunately, that relief wasn't for the reason Tess had hoped—not because he finally believed she wasn't pregnant. As became evident when he asked, "Then at least it was someone you cared about?"

Argh, she thought eloquently. Just what was it going to take to dislodge this misconception of her pregnancy from his brain? "It was the hotel repairman, Will," she said through gritted teeth.

"What?" he cried. "You slept with the hotel repairman? Tess, I can't believe you'd do such a thing. I mean, how long did you know the guy before you...you know?"

She blew out a long, exasperated breath. Great. Now they were back to her loose morals.

"I didn't say the hotel repairman is the baby's father," Tess corrected mildly. "He was just the man in my hotel room that your unidentified 'someone' saw."

Will's outrage cooled and was immediately replaced by confusion. "Then who's the baby's father?" he asked.

Tess shook her head, growing weary. "How many times do I have to tell you, Will? *There is no father.*"

He eyed her warningly, cautiously. "No father?" he echoed dubiously. "You know, you oughta be careful, Tess. I'm not sure, but you could be blaspheming here. Have you talked to Father Flynn about all this yet?"

She rolled her eyes heavenward and somehow refrained from wrapping her fingers around his throat. "Will, there is no father because there is *no baby.*"

At that the color drained right out of his face. "Tess, no," he said in a shallow voice. "Tell me you didn't do something drastic. Tell me you didn't do anything to the baby. Tell me you didn't—"

Her eyes went wide when she understood what he was suggesting. "Of *course* I didn't do anything to the baby," she gasped, her shock almost palpable. "I would *never*...I could *never*..."

He exhaled a long sigh of relief. "Oh, thank God."

This had gone way too far, Tess thought, had gotten way, way, *way* out of hand. She took a moment to try and reel in her thoughts, inhaled deeply a few times to clear her brain, then sighed with much frustration.

"The man in my room," she finally said, "was the hotel repairman. He wasn't there to have sex with me," she added quickly when she saw Will ready to interrupt, "he was there to fix the air conditioner."

Will's expression shifted to faint—very faint—credulity. "The air conditioner?"

"The air conditioner," she repeated. She continued slowly, deliberately, as if she were speaking to a three-year-old child. Hey, if Will was going to act like one, then he deserved to be treated like one. "The air conditioner in my room wasn't working," she began in her best once-upon-a-time voice. "They sent a guy to fix it. It took him over an hour to get it done, but that's what that was all about."

Will's expression didn't change. "It was March, Tess. Why did you need the air conditioner?"

She closed her eyes, praying for patience. "It was a warm day," she said. "The room was stuffy."

He looked nowhere near convinced. "What about Bonnie's Baby Boutique?" he asked.

Tess narrowed her eyes at him, her head spinning from the sudden jump to a new track. "What about it?"

"Word has it you made a big purchase there not long ago."

"Yeah, I did," she admitted. "So?"

"So why would you be buying baby stuff if you're not pregnant?"

"Not that it's any of your business," she replied coolly, "or anyone else's for that matter, but I have four on-line friends who are pregnant. I wanted to send a little something to each of them to say congrats."

Of this he was obviously skeptical. "On-line friends?" he repeated blandly.

Tess nodded.

"You're on-line that much?"

She shrugged. "I'm on a lot of list servs."

"List servs?"

Tess ticked them off on her fingers. "One for gardening, one for romance novels, one for first-grade teachers, one for genealogy, one for movies—"

"Jeez, Tess, just how much time do you spend on-line?" Will interjected.

Well, what else was she supposed to do? she wanted to ask him. Marigold was a small town, and it wasn't exactly overflowing with social opportunities. And even if it *was* overflowing with social opportunities, nobody was asking Tess to any of them. And even if someone *did* ask Tess to one of them, she wasn't likely to go. Not unless it was Will Darrow doing the asking.

And that wasn't likely, was it?

"I don't spend all that much time on-line," she said defensively. "A couple of hours a night, a few nights a week. But that's what the purchases at Bonnie's were for."

He hesitated only a moment before charging, "You don't own a computer, Tess."

"No, but the library's on-line," she pointed out.

He was looking at her in a way that made her think he wanted to ask if she had any postal receipts to back up her assertion. Instead he asked, "What about the...uh...the, um... I mean... Somebody said you..."

"What?" Tess demanded. Snappishly, too, because she was getting really impatient with this interrogation.

Will sighed fitfully. "Somebody said you went to see a...uh... They said you saw a, um..."

"Will!" she ground out, exasperated. "Who? Who did I go to see?"

"The, uh...the doctor," he finally finished. "Somebody said that you went to see...you know...one of...*those*...doctors."

By now Tess was getting pretty tired of having her veracity questioned, her privacy intruded upon and her dignity insulted. So, just to be vexatious, realizing how uncomfortable he was with the very subject he'd brought up, she said emphatically, "Do you mean the *gynecologist*, Will?"

He flinched as if she had just physically struck him. "Yeah," he said softly. "One of those. Somebody said they saw you at the...um... That they saw you...there."

Tess nodded. "It's really interesting, you know, but every time I go to the *gynecologist*—" she took perverse pleasure in seeing him squeeze his eyes shut tight "—I see *a lot* of women there. It's the oddest thing. Why do you think that is, Will? That so many women go to see a *gynecologist?*"

"Look, just answer the question," he said as he opened his eyes again, obviously no happier with the new conversational route they'd traveled down than she was.

Still, he was the one who'd guided them this way, wasn't he?

"There was no question, Will," Tess pointed out, crossing her arms over her abdomen. "I don't have to answer anything. None of this is any of your business."

He blew out an impatient breath and ran a hand through his dark hair, none too gently. "Look, did you go to see the...doctor...or not?"

"Yes," she said. "I went to see the *gynecologist*. And you know what, Will? I'll do it again. I'll do it annually. How do you like them apples?"

"You went twice in two months' time," he charged, ignoring her sarcasm.

Tess's mouth dropped open in astonishment. Was *nothing* sacred? Were there no bounds to the lengths that people would go to in order to perpetuate and embellish a rumor? "Boy, how do people find out about all this stuff?" she wondered aloud. "Do they have nothing better to do? Don't they have any hobbies? They should go on-line. It would keep them off the streets and out of rumor mills."

"Tess," Will said softly. "Just give it up. Nobody believes you when you say you're not pregnant. And we're all here for you. Nobody's going to think less of you for what's happened. We all make mistakes."

When she glanced up at his face, she was surprised to see that Will was, in fact, meeting her gaze squarely, for the first time in years. What was even more surprising was the fact that he was obviously genuinely concerned about her. Although he had made up his mind about her condition, he wasn't judging her. He was worried about her, that was all. It was actually kind of sweet.

Or, rather, it would have been kind of sweet. If she were really pregnant.

"Will," she said softly, one final time, "I'm *not* pregnant."

"Then tell me why you made such frequent trips to see the...doctor."

There was no way—*no way*—that Tess was going to discuss her recent yeast infection with anyone, certainly not with Will Darrow. She didn't care if it meant the Marigold grapevine had her carrying sextuplets by week's end. Some things were just too private to reveal to a man who wasn't one's husband. Especially since the yeast infection hadn't recurred.

"I can't tell you that," she said softly.

His entire body slumped forward in response, and Tess knew then that she'd lost him. Not that she'd ever really had him to begin with, she reminded herself. But she had rather hoped that Will might at least give her the benefit of the doubt. Her brothers, she knew, were a lost cause. Once the Monahan boys made up their minds about something, there was no changing those minds without irrefutable evidence to back her up. But Will... Will had always seemed so reasonable, so open-minded. And she honestly hadn't thought he would be capable of thinking the worst of her.

"Tess," he said, the single word laced with dark disappointment. But no other words followed. Not that any were necessary. His expression told her everything she needed to know. Even giving him the real reason she'd been to the gynecologist wasn't likely to alter his conviction. Like everyone else in town, Will Darrow was a victim of the Marigold rumor mill.

May God have mercy on his soul.

No amount of denying the gossip was likely to have an effect, Tess thought. Not on Will, not on anybody. Certainly she *would* keep denying the charges, and, of course, she would do everything she could to dissuade everybody of their belief. But deep down she knew it was going to take time before anybody believed her. Probably about six or seven months, to be exact. All Tess could do now was wait it out and make the best of a bad situation.

She just wished she wouldn't have to do it alone.

Four

Will Darrow studied Tess Monahan's face in the splash of yellow lamplight that spilled from behind her, with two thoughts warring in his head at the same time. Number one, he was thinking about what an incredibly beautiful woman she had become. And number two, he was thinking about how he wished with all his heart that he could believe her when she said she wasn't pregnant.

But what was he supposed to do? There was so much evidence against her. Okay, *maybe* he could buy the repairman thing, but she'd been up in Bloomington in March—not exactly the season for air-conditioning. And she'd never been sick in her life—only something alien to her system, like morning sickness, could bring about such a reaction. And, yeah, the local library was on-line, but still. And she never had told him why she'd been to see the…doctor…twice, in so short a time. Women only went to the…doctor…annually, as Tess herself had pointed out. Unless they had some other condition that warranted such a thing. Like pregnancy.

Although Tess wasn't the kind of person to tell a lie, in this situation, he could see her panicking and acting out of character. Marigold, Indiana, was a small, tightly knit, conservative community. Even though Will couldn't imagine anybody turning their back on Tess for something like this, she might very well worry that people would.

Plus, her five older brothers were notorious for pounding anyone who challenged the good name of Monahan. Not that they'd ever harm a hair on Tess's head—they doted on her totally—but they'd make mincemeat out of anyone who gave their kid sister a hard time. And they'd beat the hell out of anyone who knocked their kid sister up. All in all, Will could definitely see Tess denying the rumors of her condition, if for no other reason than to keep the peace for as long as she could.

Because that was the kind of person she was—she didn't want to cause trouble for anybody. She hated to see turmoil in anybody's life. And fear made a person react in funny ways. God knew she must be scared, being pregnant and single and living in a town like Marigold, where everybody knew everybody else's business. Hell, he'd probably be denying it, too, if he were in her position.

Still feeling confused and ragged about everything, Will arced his gaze around the room, then felt his heart plummet at what he saw there—a deconstructed crib, a tiny cradle, a bag overflowing with toys and a stack of boxes in the corner. The top one didn't have any flaps, and he could see that it was filled with clothes. Clothes in soft pinks, pale blues and pastel yellows. Baby colors.

Baby clothes?

Of course, Tess wore a lot of those colors herself.... Involuntarily his gaze went back to her current—pale-blue—outfit, and he wished like hell it hadn't. Because her brief T-shirt wasn't quite loose enough to keep him from noticing that she wasn't wearing a bra, and her pajama bottoms rode a little low on her hips, revealing a generous ribbon of creamy flesh between the two garments.

Dammit, he wished he could stop looking at that creamy ribbon of flesh.

He snatched his gaze away, and before he even realized he'd intended to go anywhere, he found himself standing beside the box, extracting what appeared to be a little pink sleeper-thing with a fuzzy bunny sewn on the front. Nope. Definitely not Tess's size.

"You wanna explain this?" he asked. He swept his arm around the room. "You wanna explain all of this to me, Tess?" he added, meeting her gaze once more. "'Cause I gotta tell ya, if you're not pregnant, then I don't understand any of it."

She dropped her face into her hands, though whether the action was caused by frustration or embarrassment or shame or anger, he couldn't say for sure.

"Tess?" he spurred.

She lifted her head then, even higher than usual, really, and gazed at him in utter defiance. "I think you better go," she told him. "There's no point in us discussing this any further."

He swallowed hard, irrational anger eating at him from the inside out. Strangely, though, he was more upset about her easy dismissal of him than he was about anything else. There had been a time in the past when Tess Monahan would have given anything to be in the same room with him. There had been a time when she had followed him around like a lovesick puppy. Now, clearly, someone else had taken his place in her heart. Because not only was she telling Will to leave her home, she was carrying another man's child in her womb.

The phrasing of that thought hit him square upside the head, and he marveled that he would categorize the father of Tess Monahan's baby as "another man." Will had never been Tess Monahan's man to begin with. Oh, he'd thought it was kind of sweet, the way she'd trailed after him when she was a young girl with ratty hair and grass-stained blue jeans experiencing her first romantic crush. But Will was ten years older than Tess. She'd never been more to him than just a kid.

Not until she'd come home from IU with her newly minted master's degree looking like…like…like… Well, *not* like a kid. It was as if Tess had left Marigold a skinny seventeen-year-old girl with bad skin and no curves, and had come home five years later from Bloomington looking like…like…like…

Wow.

That's what she'd come home looking like. And ever since then, Will's feelings toward her had been a strange and tangled mix of wanting to protect her and wanting to be exactly the kind of guy she needed protection from. And frankly, that pretty much scared the hell out of him.

Because whenever he found himself in the same room with her—like right now, for instance—he just got all…hot. All over. All the time. And the last thing Will needed to be was hot for his best friend's kid sister. That was just too weird. Plus, if Finn ever found out about the licentious thoughts Will had been having about his kid sister, Finn would kick his ass.

Even so, now Tess was twenty-six, and there was no mistaking that she was a woman. But there was still something so innocent about her, something so ingenuous, something so...pure. Her current condition didn't change that. As far as Will was concerned, she was still a sweet, innocent kid...who just so happened to look like a beautiful, tempting, ripe...arousing...vivacious... luscious—oh, boy, was she luscious—delectable... mouthwatering...

Uh, where was he? Oh, yeah.

A sweet, innocent kid, who looked like a beautiful, tempting woman. And if that wasn't a combination to drive most men to madness, Will didn't know what was.

But it would be nothing but trouble to pursue anything with his best friend's kid sister. Not that there was anything to pursue, anyway, he reminded himself. Just because Tess had told him a few years ago—under the influence of Mrs. Monahan's infamous Pink Parisian Punch—that she'd always had a raging crush on him, well, that didn't mean anything. And just because his initial reaction—which he had most definitely curbed— to her confession back then had been to lunge forward, rope his arms around her, cover her mouth with his and consume her in one, big, voracious bite, well, that had just been a reaction to Mrs. Monahan's infamous Pink Parisian Punch.

Hadn't it?

Of course it had.

Now Tess was pregnant with another man's child, so any confessions—or curbed reactions to confessions— were totally immaterial. It didn't matter how fresh they were in Will's memory. And it didn't matter how much he regretted running off that day, instead of hanging around to explore the potential...*after* lunging forward, roping his arms around her, covering her mouth with his and consuming her in one, big, voracious bite.

Tess Monahan was pregnant. With another man's child. And Will would just have to deal with it.

"I mean it, Will," she said, bringing his thoughts back to the matter at hand. "I want you to leave. If you can't even accept my word that the rumors are untrue, then I don't want you in my house."

Point taken, he thought.

Without a further word, he spun on his heel and headed for the front door. Because he couldn't quite bring himself to accept Tess's word that the rumors were untrue. There was just too much talk going on. There were too many things that didn't add up. Her explanations were flimsy, she was behaving strangely, and he could see for himself that something had her looking tired and frail.

And Tess Monahan just wasn't a tired, frail person. She also wouldn't need an air conditioner repairman in March. She also didn't own a computer to be on-line as often as she said she was. And she never, ever, got sick. In spite of that she'd been to see a...doctor...twice in two months' time.

Put it all together, it spelled *pregnant*.

Tess Monahan pregnant, Will thought again as he opened the front door and strode with much preoccupation and confusion into the balmy spring evening. Just what the hell was the world coming to?

By the time school let out for the summer that second week in June, Marigold, Indiana, was in full bloom. Lush canopies of maple and oak spanned the streets, the parks were brimming with green space and activity, rose bushes burst into reds and pinks and yellows along the avenues, the skies were blue, blue, blue and utterly limitless, and...

...and Tess Monahan had completely given up denying

allegations that she was pregnant. During the past month, she had swayed absolutely no one in her continuous efforts to change the opinions of the residents of Marigold. To them, she was going to have a baby. Period. End of story. There was nothing to do now but wait it out and prove to them there was no baby for her to have.

So now whenever someone congratulated her on the upcoming blessed event, she only smiled weakly, murmured her thanks and continued on her way.

Whenever someone stopped by her house with a box full of baby or maternity clothes, she only smiled weakly, murmured her thanks and added the contribution to her growing collection in the basement.

Whenever one of the local librarians pulled a baby or pregnancy book from the reserved shelf, where they'd all taken the liberty of placing them on Tess's behalf, she only smiled weakly, murmured her thanks and dropped the book to the top of her stack.

She had surrendered any and all hopes of countering anyone's speculation about her condition. Nobody was really giving her a hard time, after all, and everyone seemed to be genuinely excited about the upcoming—if fictional—birth. There were times when Tess almost felt guilty for *not* being pregnant, so happy did everyone seem to be about it.

Even her own family was dealing surprisingly well with the nondevelopment. Her parents—now that they had gotten over their initial shock upon hearing about her condition from Finn—were far from feeling ashamed about their daughter's sudden moral lapse, nor were they worried about her raising a child alone. In fact, they were both very excited about the arrival of their first grandchild and had sent a lovely, hand-knit sweater for Tess to add to her nonexistent baby's layette. Her brothers, too, broke out in goofy grins whenever mention was made of the fact that they were about to become uncles.

Except, of course, for Finn. Finn was much too focused on giving the baby's father a relentless pounding—after which he would force the baby's father to propose marriage—the minute Tess revealed who it might be. In the meantime he had launched a campaign to discern paternal identity in whatever way he could manage. So far, though, much to his frustration, Finn had come up empty.

For a full month now, such had been Tess's lot in life. She'd tolerated the town of Marigold's incessant chatter about her pregnancy and their ceaseless efforts to help her in whatever ways they could. And she knew she would be tolerating it for some time to come, until enough time passed that everyone could see that she *wasn't* pregnant. She tolerated it because she had no choice.

What she *couldn't* tolerate much longer, however, was the constant speculation about her imaginary baby's non-existent father.

And although such speculation had been veiled in the nicest, most polite terms possible—so far—it had still been present. All the time. The hinting had started off innocently enough, but was gradually becoming more and more blatant.

"Oh, Tess. You and the baby's *father* must be so excited" followed by the expectant look.

Or "Tess! So good to see you getting over that awful morning sickness. The baby's *father* must be relieved, too" followed by the encouraging nod. *And* the expectant look.

Or "Tess Monahan, you're absolutely glowing. I'll bet the baby's *father* can't keep his hands to himself these days'' followed by the playful nudge. *And* the expectant look. *And* the encouraging nod.

It wouldn't be long before people were simply stopping her on the street and saying, ''All right, Tess. Who is he?'' And then where would she be? Ignoring silent suggestiveness was easy enough to do and still maintain a polite veneer. But how was she supposed to answer honestly a point-blank interrogation? Then again, what was the point in answering honestly? she often asked herself. Nobody believed her when she did.

It was going to be a long summer.

Which was made all the more evident that second week in June, when Tess was standing in line at Marigold's new supermarket, and the very situation she feared finally arose. She had filled her shopping cart with her usual healthful fare—fresh produce, pasta, skim milk, et cetera—and was waiting to check out, flipping through one of those impulse-buy minibooklets about controlling weight gain, when Nancy Rosen pushed her cart into line right behind her.

''Give it up, Tess,'' Nancy said when she noted Tess's choice of reading material. ''You're going to blow up like a balloon—there's nothing you can do to stop it.''

Tess turned to throw her redheaded neighbor a cool look. ''I beg your pardon?'' she said, hoping the other woman might get the point and keep her opinions to herself.

Fat chance. So to speak.

''I said,'' Nancy reiterated, ''that you're going to blow up like a balloon while you're pregnant, so don't even bother to try watching your weight.''

Instead of denying that she was pregnant—it was, after all, pointless—Tess sidestepped the matter by replying,

"My diet hasn't changed one iota in the past four years. Why would I blow up like anything?"

Nancy smiled. "One word. Cravings. Have you had any yet?"

"No," Tess replied. Honestly, too.

"Well, brace yourself," Nancy said. "Mine got totally out of control when I was pregnant with Stephanie. And with Christopher..." She waved a hand airily in front of her. "All I wanted for seven months was Neapolitan ice cream and prosciutto."

"Well. At least you got your calcium and protein," Tess said. Honestly.

"Yeah, and thighs the size of Rhode Island," Nancy countered. "Even after losing the added weight, my body just ain't the one I had before I got preggers. Kiss those perky little breasts goodbye, kiddo."

Tess squeezed her eyes shut tight. Nancy Rosen had never been known for her tact and courtesy in the first place, but neither was she a woman known for malicious chatter. There was one thing Tess was discovering about being pregnant—even if she *wasn't* pregnant. Women who'd given birth themselves took great delight in sharing the war stories of their own pregnancies. Stretch marks, in particular, seemed to be great badges of honor.

"And the *stretch marks*," Nancy added. "Oh, my God. You can't imagine."

Tess smiled weakly, saw with much relief that it was her turn to unload her cart, so spun around and hoped that would be an end to the conversation with Nancy.

No such luck.

"So, Tess," the other woman said as she inched her own cart forward, "have you signed up for childbirth classes yet? With some of those methods, you need to start early. And, of course, you'll want to register the baby's *father* as your partner.''

Tess glanced up from her task to find that the comment was, inescapably, followed by an expectant look. And an encouraging nod. Had she been closer, she was certain Nancy would have punctuated the remark with a playful nudge, as well.

''Mmm,'' Tess replied noncommittally. And, as always, she ignored the reference to the baby's *father*.

Until Nancy continued, ''Just who is the baby's father, anyway? We're all dying to know.''

Okay. That did it. The time had come. Tess had finally, finally reached the end of her rope. Nobody would believe her when she said she *wasn't* pregnant. Nobody would believe her *at all* when she tried to tell the truth. And frankly, she was sick and tired of it. As far as she was concerned, she couldn't be held responsible for her actions after this. The people of Marigold had driven her to it.

So, impulsively, she told Nancy, ''You don't know the baby's father. He's not from Marigold.''

Nancy's expression grew fairly rabid at this little snippet of new information for the Marigold grapevine. ''Well, then...when will we get to meet him?'' she asked.

Tess reached into her basket for a cantaloupe, thought for a moment longer, then told Nancy, ''You won't be meeting him. In fact, I'll probably never see him again myself.''

The other woman gaped almost comically for a moment, then, ''Why not?'' she asked.

Tess sighed tragically. ''Because he's in the Witness Protection Program.''

Nancy's eyes went as wide as saucers. ''He's *what?*''

Tess turned her attention back to unloading her groceries. "He's in the Witness Protection Program," she repeated mildly, grinning to herself. "He used to be connected to the Mob," she continued blithely, warming to the newly minted history of her former—nonexistent— lover, "but after he met me, he saw the error of his ways and went good. Then he turned state's evidence. Now there's a contract on his head, so he's had to go into the Witness Protection Program. He's probably selling shoes somewhere in Idaho by now. He doesn't even know I'm pregnant. It's a secret baby." Just for good measure she dropped a hand over her belly and sighed again, even more tragically than before. "It's so sad. Our baby will grow up never knowing its father."

Tess was sure she had piled it on thick enough that Nancy would know she was being sarcastic, and for a moment the other woman did look skeptical. Then, "Oh, *Tess,*" she said in a crushed voice, extending a hand forward. "I'm so, so sorry. That is so, so sad. Your poor baby. That poor little fatherless child."

This time Tess was the one to gape comically, and for a moment she had no idea what to say. Nancy believed her? She actually *believed* that ridiculous tale? Here Tess could tell the truth about her nonexistent baby's nonpaternity until she was blue in the face, and nobody would accept a word of it. But, hey, weave a great whopping lie that was totally outrageous, and *now* someone thought she was telling the truth?

Incredible.

"Nancy, don't—"

But the other woman held up a hand to cut her off. "*I won't tell a soul, Tess,*" she vowed ominously. "I can see how this would make for a delicate situation."

"But, Nancy—"

"And you can count on me and Ed to be there for you, if you need anything. You just let us know."

"But, Nancy—"

"The Witness Protection Program…I can't imagine."

"But—"

"I mean, that only happens on TV, you know? And you have no idea where he is? He doesn't even know about the baby? It's just so tragic."

Tess tried a half dozen more times to sway Nancy from her thinking, to absolutely no avail. Then the cashier barked out her total, and Tess glanced up to see the young girl gazing at her in much the same way Nancy was. As if she *wouldn't tell a soul,* either. Worse still, just beyond the cashier, in the next aisle, stood none other than Will Darrow. And he, too, was gazing at Tess with an expression of utter shock…but *not* disbelief.

She closed her eyes and expelled a long, frustrated groan. Was there anything that could possibly make this day worse than it already was? She opened her eyes to find that Will had paid for his purchase and was striding around the counter toward her. And she thought, Yep. There most definitely was something that could make the day worse than it already was.

Five

The Witness Protection Program? Will reiterated to himself as he paid the cashier for his meager purchase. *The Witness Protection Program?* A former mobster? A contract on his head? The revelations about the father of Tess's baby rocked Will to the very core of his existence. Jeez, no wonder she didn't want to talk about her pregnancy. The poor kid was probably mired in denial. Who wouldn't be, under circumstances like that? She was probably scared to death.

She was such an innocent, he thought further. Such a sweet, kind, decent person. How the hell could she have gotten involved with some scumbag mobster? Well, it was probably because she *was* such a sweet, kind, decent person, of course. Scumbags were always taking advantage of people like Tess.

It must have happened when she was up in Bloomington—things like that happened in the big city all the time, didn't they? And, hey, it didn't matter if her inherent sweetness, kindness and decency had rubbed off on the guy or not. It was all well and good that he'd turned away from the dark side and had helped convict the riffraff he was running around with. But he'd gotten Tess in trouble in the process. He'd gotten her pregnant. Will could only thank God that the guy hadn't dragged her down any further than he had.

The Witness Protection Program, he marveled yet again. Then an even more terrible thought struck him. What if the baby's father had tried to take Tess into hiding with him? Will might never have seen her again. Or, rather, the Monahans might never have seen her again. Or what if the guy found out about the baby and came looking for Tess now? What if she ran off with him? What if she just up and disappeared one day? Will...or rather, the Monahans...would never get over it.

Ah, hell. He might as well admit it. He'd never get over it, either.

Tess was just so much a part of Marigold, so much a part of his own personal history. It was only natural that he would miss her if she disappeared. She'd always been like a kid sister to him. Well, until she'd come home from college looking like anything *but* a kid. Until the feelings he had for her had become anything *but* brotherly.

He collected his change and thanked the cashier, then hefted up the paper sack he'd filled with the basic necessities of masculine life—boxed macaroni and cheese, frozen pizza rolls, a bunch of bananas, that kind of thing; Will prided himself on his low-maintenance diet. Then he turned to find that Tess was placing the last of her purchases into her own paper sack.

Without even thinking about what he was doing, he rounded the checkout counter and dropped his bag into the cart alongside the rest of hers, then lifted the one she was picking up and added it to the collection.

"You don't need to be lifting heavy things," he said to explain his proprietary gesture.

She blew out a breath that sounded vaguely exasperated. "It's not heavy," she denied.

And thankfully, that was all she denied. She'd begun to look kind of pathetic, the way she'd kept trying to convince everybody in Marigold that she wasn't pregnant, when everybody in Marigold knew that she was. Now, thankfully, it looked like she was starting to come clean with details about the baby's father—it was a good sign that she was finally beginning to accept the particulars of her situation.

Of course, the details she was coming clean *with* weren't particularly clean, he recalled with another one of those odd waves of nausea. But it was something.

"That's beside the point," he told her. "You need to be careful in your condition. You need to have somebody around who can help you out. Especially since it looks like the baby's father *isn't* going to be around for you."

She expelled another one of those impatient sounds and said, strangely, "Well, at least you put the emphasis on some word other than *father.*"

He was about to ask her what she'd meant by that, but Tess curled her fingers around the handle of the shopping cart and purposefully guided it forward. Will immediately followed, though whether it was because his groceries were in there with hers—or for some other reason he would be better off not dwelling on at the moment—he couldn't be sure. As he caught up to her, though, he orchestrated his movements to gently nudge her aside and took over the driving for her.

"Where are you parked?" he asked before she had a

chance to challenge him…but after another one of those exasperated sounds.

She frowned, but didn't press the issue. "Toward the back of the lot. I like to walk."

He nodded his approval. "That's a good idea. Get some exercise for the baby."

"It's exercise for *me*," she said.

"Whatever," he replied softly.

He smiled inwardly. Actually, it wasn't pathetic the way she kept denying her condition, he decided. What it really was was kind of cute. *She* was kind of cute. In fact, she was very cute. Pregnancy agreed with her—that was a clear enough fact. Now that her morning sickness was obviously over, she was looking as healthy and lively as ever.

In fact, she was blushing, he noted with a smile. The warm summer breeze lifted her hair and tossed it playfully back over her shoulders, and her pale blue eyes seemed even brighter than usual. Her light-yellow shorts and oversize white T-shirt indicated she would probably be spending the day at home, and, out of nowhere, Will wondered if she needed any help getting the house ready for the baby's arrival.

Ah, well, he told himself. Time enough for that. First things first. Like working out this missing-father business, for one.

"So the baby's father is in the Witness Protection Program, huh?" Will said. Hey, no sense beating around the bush.

She halted in her tracks, and it took him a few seconds to realize she wasn't accompanying him anymore. When he turned around, it was to find her standing with her hands fisted on her hips, glaring at him.

"Don't tell me it's none of my business," he said

when he saw her expression, already anticipating her response. "Because it won't wash."

She hesitated a moment before asking, "How do you figure?"

Will hesitated not at all. "Because I care about you, Tess. I care about what happens to you. You're like a..." Ah, hell. He couldn't lie and say she was like a sister, when that was the last thing she felt like to him. "You're a good friend," he amended, though that didn't feel quite right, either. "And since the baby's father isn't around, you're going to need someone to lean on in the months ahead.

"In the *years* ahead," he amended. "It's not going to be easy raising that baby alone. I know you're close to your family, but I also know your family can be a little overwhelming at times, because they love you so much. I just want to make sure you know..." He shrugged, suddenly feeling a little uncomfortable with the direction into which this conversation had turned.

"Make sure I know what?" she prodded him.

He tried to look her in the eye, but his gaze glanced off hers as he continued, "Just that...I'm here for you. You know. If you need anything."

She started walking again, albeit more slowly this time, but once she caught up to him, she kept right on going. "I can take care of myself," she said as she passed him. "I'll be fine."

"Easy for you to say now," Will countered, wheeling the cart faster to catch up with her. "But in a few months you might feel differently."

"In a few months we'll all feel differently," she told him.

He supposed that was true. The closer it came to the baby's arrival, the more anxious they were all going to be. He took a moment and tried to imagine Tess big with child, but the image wouldn't take hold in his brain. She was such a tiny thing. He just couldn't picture her waddling around with a beach-ball-size belly.

"If you need anything, Tess," he said, a little more softly, "you just call, you hear? I know Finn and Sean and everybody have told you the same thing, but I also know how tense the Monahan family situations can get. If you don't feel like you can call one of your brothers, then you call me."

She didn't look at him when he made the offer, but Will knew she'd heard, because she started to blush again. Figuring he would be better off not pressing his luck, and having pretty much said his piece, anyway, he continued on in silence. As did Tess. But as they approached the outer edge of the parking lot and reached her car, it quickly became obvious that she'd be getting a lot more exercise today than she'd initially anticipated. Because her left rear tire was flat.

"Oh, no," she groaned. "How did that happen? I just got new tires."

And that was something to which Will himself could attest, because he'd been the one who put those tires on her car. He always made it a point to remind Tess when she needed new radials, and when she needed to have them rotated, and when it was time to come in for chains. Marigold didn't get heaps of snow in the winter, but he didn't want to take any chances. Not with Tess. Not with any of the Monahans, he quickly corrected himself.

"You're in luck," he told her.

"Doesn't look like it from where I'm standing," she muttered, still eyeing the limp tire.

"No, really," he said. "I just so happen to know a guy who owns a garage."

That, finally, made her smile. And even though the sun was shining overhead, when Tess turned to look at Will, somehow, in that moment, his day got brighter, got warmer.

"No kidding," she said.

He nodded. "And he just so happens to be driving around in his tow truck today. So he can give you a lift over to his garage, where he will gladly see to that tire, pronto."

"I guess it pays to know someone in the business," she said.

Will smiled. It certainly did.

It had been a long time since Tess had visited Darrow's Garage in more than a just passing by way, Will recalled nearly an hour later. But back when she was a kid, she'd been a frequent enough companion. She'd always stopped by after school, because it was on the way home, to chat with him and Finn and crawl under the cars to find out how they worked. For a long time Will had halfway expected that she would grow up to become a mechanic herself, she'd been that fascinated with machinery.

Now as he snapped her hubcap back into place over her new tire, he tried to remember exactly how long it had been since her last long visit, but he came up blank. Not since she'd come back from college, that was for sure. Not since she'd, you know, turned into a…woman. Will just didn't bring women to his garage. Not on purpose, anyway. Not by choice. In his case his garage was his castle, because he lived in an apartment over the bays. And Will just wasn't in the habit of bringing women to his castle.

In spite of that, after he and Tess had arrived, he'd sent

her right up to his place. Only so she could stow her perishable groceries in his refrigerator, he reminded himself quickly. Not because... Well. Not because of anything else. He just hadn't wanted anything to go bad on her—it might hurt the baby for her to eat something that went bad.

Plus, remembering her condition, he'd figured she might want to rest while he was replacing the tire on her car with a brand-spanking-new one. No tire patchwork for Tess Monahan, no way. Will wasn't about to risk that. A new tire was definitely in order. It was the least he could do for selling her a defective one—at his cost, naturally—in the first place. He would just eat the expense and write it off as a loss. Better that than lose Tess.

Tess, whom he had actually instructed to go up to his apartment, he recalled again with no small marvel. What was even more amazing was that something about having her up there felt strangely natural to Will. Oddly right. Remarkably perfect. It probably would have scared the hell out of him if it hadn't felt so good. After all, he was always *very* uncomfortable—and not a little scared—whenever Abigail Torrance, or any other woman of his acquaintance, came around. But with Tess, for some reason, that wasn't the case at all.

"How's it coming?"

The question—or maybe it was the simple sound of her voice—had Will, still squatting by her new tire, spinning around fast enough to land ignobly on his butt. His indignity, however, evaporated when he saw Tess framed in the doorway of his office. A spill of sunlight splashed around her, giving him the impression that the warmth and illumination were emanating from within her. Or maybe it was just her pregnancy that made her look that way, he further speculated.

Or maybe it was something else he'd be better off not thinking about.

Something that—who knew why?—must have made him smile, because Tess smiled in return, albeit a bit puzzled, and asked, "What's so funny?"

Will shook his head, but couldn't make himself stop grinning. "Nothing. I was just thinking about something, that's all."

"About what?"

About how good it feels to have you here, he thought before he could stop himself. Strangely, though, the realization didn't scare him as much as it probably should have. "About how hungry I am," he said instead—honestly, he was surprised to discover.

Her expression grew more puzzled. "And being hungry makes you smile?"

He shrugged. "Sometimes. Depends on what I'm hungry for." Before she could respond to that cryptic comment—Will knew it was cryptic, because he sure as hell didn't understand it—he asked her, "You want to go grab a bite to eat?" Which was *really* cryptic, because he hadn't planned on saying that at all.

But before he could take back the invitation—not that he necessarily wanted to take it back, he was astonished to realize—Tess slowly nodded her head and, even more slowly, replied, "Um, yeah. Uh, sure. O-okay." And the expression that crossed her face then went way beyond puzzled. In fact, she looked like someone had just whacked her upside the head with a two-by-four.

Totally dazed—that was the only way Will could think to describe it. Which actually might not be such a bad thing, because *totally dazed* also described how he was feeling at the moment. What on earth had made him ask Tess if she wanted to go get a bite to eat? he wondered.

Okay, so he really was hungry, and it really was coming up on dinnertime, and the thought of spending more time with her really was kind of appealing, and...

Well, that was all beside the point.

The point was that he wasn't acting like himself at all today. And he wasn't sure if that was a good thing or not. Nor could he understand why the change had come about in the first place. Then again, what difference did it make? he asked himself. All he'd done was extend an innocent invitation to Tess, and she'd accepted. What was the big deal? They both had to eat, right? Right.

"Don't you have to work, though?" she asked.

It was the perfect opportunity to back out, Will thought. He could smack his forehead and say, Oh, I forgot, and that would be the end of it.

Instead, he said, "Nah. Benjy's around here somewhere. He can pull the last hour by himself and close up shop."

Tess nodded, smiling a shy smile unlike any Will had ever seen from her. And way deep down inside himself, he felt something go *vroooom*.

"But I'll have to go home and change my clothes first," she told him. "I can't go out anywhere looking like this."

Will thought her remark odd, because as far as he was concerned, Tess looked pretty damned good at the moment, all bright-eyed and bare legs, and sun-kissed and bare legs, and wind-tossed and bare legs, and bare legs and bare legs, and—

"Um, yeah. Okay. Whatever." Maybe her changing clothes wouldn't be such a bad idea after all.

Jeez, what the hell had gotten into him? Will wondered when he realized where his attention lay. Immediately, he snatched his gaze away from her bare legs and forced it up toward her face. Unfortunately, on the way he noticed how the scooped neck of her T-shirt had dipped slightly down over one shoulder, baring the strap of her undershirt beneath.

The moment he saw it, he felt a spark of heat ignite in his belly, and with no small effort he drove his gaze upward again. That, however, just left him looking at her mouth, and quite a nice mouth it was, too, all full and ripe and dewy, her lips parted just fractionally, as if she wasn't quite getting enough air, or because she wanted somebody to come along and kiss her tenderly, or maybe not so tenderly, maybe hungrily and possessively and—

Dammit, where was his mind today? Besides the gutter, anyway.

With no small effort—but with much concentration—Will managed to steer his gaze higher still, meeting Tess's as levelly as he could. But the moment he noted the expression on her face, he realized she knew exactly what he'd been thinking—and looking at—over the last several seconds. Not only was she blushing furiously—again—but the look in her eyes told him in no uncertain terms that she didn't exactly mind his perusal. That, in fact, she wanted him to bring it closer. That she wanted to make a not-so-subtle inventory of her own.

And then it hit Will like a ton of wet diapers, what was going on. It was that…that…that hormonal thing that pregnant women experienced. Yeah, that was it. Tess's hormone levels must be skyrocketing through the roof while she was nurturing and growing that tiny life inside her. She was producing a lot of those…whaddayacall'em? Pheromones, that's it. He'd read about them in *Men's Health* magazine just last week.

Pheromones. Hey, even good little Irish-Catholic girls

like Tess Monahan had them. Will just wished she'd keep hers to herself.

But, of course, she couldn't keep them to herself, not while she was pregnant. It was one of those natural chemical reactions that was unavoidable. He was just unlucky enough to be in the vicinity when hers started firing off like cannon shots, that was all. And now, even more unluckily, by inviting her to dinner, he'd just made sure that he'd be in the vicinity of her pheromones all evening.

Fortunately for Will, though, he wasn't susceptible to pheromones. Not really. Not much. Not Tess Monahan's, anyway. Because, hey, he could remember when Tess Monahan was just a kid without pheromones. He could remember that really well. And to prove it, he closed his eyes and roused an image of her at seven years old, barefoot with uneven braids streaming over her shoulders and two front teeth missing and wearing grubby jeans and a pink Barbie T-shirt.

Or at least he tried to rouse that image. Unfortunately, it just wouldn't come. Suddenly Will couldn't picture Tess as a child at all. The image that did emerge in his brain was the one he'd catalogued only moments ago, of a very grown-up Tess and her long, long legs, her T-shirt dipping down low on one shoulder, the strap of her undergarment peeking out from beneath.

And then that image began to shift and change, and the one that took its place was just way, *way* too troubling for Will to entertain. Because it was an image of Tess stretched out beside him in his bed, her bare shoulders revealed by the dangerously dipping sheet, her pale blond hair streaming off her pillow and onto his.

Will snapped his eyes open wide just as the image materialized, but not before it branded itself at the forefront of his brain. Even so, he did his best to dispel it.

The capital of South Dakota is Pierre. The Wizard of Oz *won thirteen Academy Awards. The chemical symbol for silver is Ag. Wisconsin is the Badger State.*

Unfortunately, no amount of trivia knowledge would dislodge the vision from his head.

Tess Monahan in his bed, he marveled. It was too weird to think about. But what was even weirder was that he *did* think about it. And what was weirder still was the fact that he realized...it wasn't such a weird thought, after all.

How weird.

"Um, Tess..."

"But you know what, Will?" she said just as he spoke up himself. In deference to her—ladies first, and all that—he halted and let her continue. "Since we're going over to my house anyway, why don't you let me make dinner for you?"

Oh, boy, how he suddenly wished he hadn't deferred and let her continue, ladies first or not.

He opened his mouth to tell her no, to voice some reason, however lame, for why they should go out someplace—someplace very public—instead. Or, better yet, to tell her he just remembered a very important appointment, and, hey, what a bummer, he was going to have to take a rain check on that meal, but hold that thought, because someday in the vague-but-not-too-distant, honest, future, he and Tess could catch that bite to eat. Really.

But when he opened his mouth to say all that, what he actually heard coming out was, "Sure, Tess. I'd love to."

And that was when Will Darrow realized that the end of the world as he knew it was definitely in sight.

Six

Sure, Tess. I'd love to.

Will's easy reply was still circling pleasantly in Tess's brain as she put the finishing touches on their dinner. Not just because of the warm, wonderful way he had said the words, but because they were words she could imagine hearing in reply to so many other questions she might want to ask him.

Will, would you pick up a gallon of milk on your way home from work today?

Sure, Tess. I'd love to.

Will, do you mind rubbing my feet? I've been on them all day.

Sure, Tess. I'd love to.

Will, could you check on the baby and make sure she's covered?

Sure, Tess. I'd love to.

Will, will you marry me?

Sure, Tess. I'd love to.

Oh, it was all just too nice to think about. And even nicer than her rich fantasy life of the past couple of hours was her current reality. Because her current reality *was* her rich fantasy life. As he had done so many times in her daydreams, Will Darrow was standing right in Tess's kitchen, leaning against the counter and keeping her company, after having set the table for the two of them.

Set the table, she marveled again. *For the two of them.*

And the whole thing was just so irresistibly domestic and cozy. Frankly, she had no idea why he had accepted her invitation to dinner—nor could she still quite believe she had extended it in the first place—but at the moment Tess didn't care. All that mattered was that Will was here. All that mattered was that they had a whole evening ahead of them to spend together, alone. And she wondered what she would have to do to make him stay forever—short of duct-taping him to one of the kitchen chairs or locking him in the basement.

"I always loved this house," he said then, stirring her from her thoughts. "There are lots of happy memories here, and it has a good soul." He smiled at her, a dreamy little smile that warmed parts of her she hadn't realized were cold. "It'll be a good place for you to raise your child, Tess."

Just like that, the warm glow dimmed, because she remembered then why Will had accepted her invitation to dinner. He thought she needed somebody around who could help her get through her pregnancy, seeing as how the nonexistent father of her imaginary baby was in the Witness Protection Program.

Boy, way to put a damper on the evening.

"It will most definitely be a good place to raise a child," she agreed halfheartedly—but honestly. The house really would be a good place to raise a child. Someday. Nestled in one of Marigold's oldest and most picturesque neighborhoods, the roomy Victorian had been in the Monahan family since it was built more than one hundred years ago.

And it was exactly the kind of house that should remain in a family forever, she thought further. Hardwood floors, high ceilings, intricate moldings and other such beautiful details were prevalent throughout. The master suite had a fireplace, and the uppermost floor, though never used for anything other than an attic, could be nicely renovated for a playroom or sitting room. There was a big backyard, complete with garden and rose trellis, a wide wraparound front porch with wicker swing, and high at the most tippy-top peak, a copper rooster weather vane.

Tess had often thought the house would make the perfect set for a Depression-era, feel-good movie. Because she'd never felt anything but good growing up here. Nothing would make her happier than raising her own child—or children—the same way. Someday.

"Which room will you use for the nursery?" Will asked further, jolting her back to her present.

She sighed and gave the spaghetti sauce one last stir, then replaced the antisplash screen to let it simmer for another twenty minutes. Will had changed out of his greasy coveralls when he'd finished with her tire, and now wore a clean pair of jeans and a navy polo embroidered with the Darrow's Garage logo. It was as dressed-up as she'd ever seen him, and she had to bite back a sigh at how handsome he looked.

So Tess, too, had changed her clothes upon arriving home, opting for a lightweight, pale yellow sundress in deference to the heat. Although the Monahan house was air-conditioned, it wasn't as well wired or insulated as it probably should be for such an extravagance, so she only ran it when the summer temperatures became unbearably hot. At the moment, a warm, rose-scented breeze pushed through the open kitchen window, fluttering the lace curtains that had hung there since before Tess was born.

"I suppose," she began—honestly—"that the best room for a nursery would be the one Finn and Sean used to share. It's the second-largest bedroom, and it overlooks the back of the house. It's bright, but still shaded from direct sunlight. And quiet. I think it would make a nice nursery."

Will nodded. "It could use some paint, though. Especially if the baby is a girl. The blue in there now is starting to look its age."

"Yes, it could use painting," Tess agreed—honestly. "But there's plenty of time for that." Especially since there wasn't likely to be child occupying that room for another four or five years, at least. Then again, the way Tess was pining for a man she was never going to have, there might never be a child occupying that room—not one of hers, at any rate.

Will shrugged off the assertion. "You know, I could take a couple of days off next week and come over and paint the room for you. Walls one day, trim the next. You probably shouldn't be around paint fumes in your condition."

Tess bit back a growl of frustration. "It's not necessary, Will," she assured him. "Summer is one of your busy seasons at work, and I don't want to take you away from that. But thank you, anyway," she added belatedly.

Again he shrugged off her remark. "Now that school's out, I have Benjy Novak and Kim Davidson helping out me and Mark at the garage—Benjy and Mark are both there full-time now. A couple days off during the week isn't going to be a problem for me, really.''

''Thanks, but it's not necessary,'' she said again.

He didn't argue the point any further, for which Tess was grateful. Then again, he didn't agree to abide by her assurance that painting wasn't necessary, either. Hmm...

It really would be nice to raise a child in this house, she thought again, pushing thoughts of paint reluctantly aside. She'd love to be able to create the kind of home that everyone in her family would want to return to, year after year, for special occasions. Eventually she was hoping to buy the house from her parents, to live here with her own husband and host all the holiday parties throughout the year. She could envision herself as a ninety-year-old woman, welcoming back her children and grandchildren and great-grandchildren to this very house for Christmas, with her husband of sixty-some years by her side.

Try as she might to envision that husband, though, there had always been only one face she could give to him. Will Darrow's. But she'd never really thought there had been any chance of that particular dream coming true.

Actually, that wasn't *quite* accurate. For one very brief, very scintillating moment this afternoon, when Will had glanced up at her in the garage, she'd almost thought he wanted to... Well. Do something to and with her that he'd never done before. Tess got hot all over again just thinking about it. She couldn't begin to imagine where that heated look had come from, but its intent had been unmistakable.

For that very brief, very scintillating moment, she had turned Will Darrow on.

And even if it had only been for a minute, it was something. Something little, granted, but still. Things had shifted between them with that look, even if only for a moment. She just wished she could say exactly *how* they had shifted. She was still feeling a little too off-kilter at the moment to try and analyze it herself.

In spite of that new dimension, however, Tess couldn't quite escape the notion that the true reason Will was here with her now *wasn't* because she'd momentarily turned him on, but because he thought she—and her baby—needed a caretaker. In spite of his heated look earlier, his real mission in coming tonight was because he was assuming the role of big brother, even though Tess already had five of those living in town.

All in all, heated looks aside, somehow she suspected she'd never be anything but little Tessie Monahan to Will. Making a pot of spaghetti for him wasn't likely to change that.

"How about some wine?" she asked impulsively.

His eyes went wide at the offer. "Wine?" he echoed. "Um, gee, I don't know, Tess. A woman in your condition and all—"

"One glass won't hurt me," she said. Honestly. *Because I'm not pregnant!* she wanted to shout further.

"But—"

"Wine will just go so nicely with the spaghetti," she pointed out. "I promise I'll just sip it and nurse one glass all night, all right?"

"Well…"

Before he had a chance to object again, Tess withdrew a nice Merlot from a small wine rack sitting on the countertop, and a corkscrew from a nearby drawer. As she worked free the cork, Will watched her with undisguised concern, as if he were gravely worried about her—no doubt because she was a pregnant woman who'd been driven to drink by the unfortunate circumstances surrounding her child's conception.

Before the cork was even free of the bottle, Tess surrendered. "All right," she muttered, setting the bottle none too gently on the counter. "I'll have a glass of milk. There's some beer in the fridge door, if you want one."

Will smiled. "Thanks. Don't mind if I do."

Tess shook her head in silent disbelief of what she had just done. She'd just agreed to drink milk on behalf of her nonexistent baby's health. At this rate she'd be knitting booties before the month was over and flipping through name books to find just the right moniker for her child.

She wondered if there was some kind of psychological condition a person could get, where they started to believe all the talk that was circulating about them—other than delusions of grandeur, anyway. Because there was certainly nothing grand about Tess's situation. Though that delusion business might not be too far off.

She tried not to think about it as she poured herself a glass of milk and debated the pros and cons of naming a boy Julian.

Will called himself six kinds of fool as he unloaded the back of his truck two days after spending a surprisingly agreeable evening with Tess. He still couldn't quite get over exactly *how* agreeable the evening had been. How *different* it had been from the evenings he usually spent with women.

Usually when he was on a date, Will was never all that comfortable. The whole man/woman thing eluded him, so he generally dealt with it by just flat-out avoiding it. He knew some guys who were smooth as silk when it came to women—Sean Monahan, for example, who could sweet-talk just about *any* woman into doing just about *any*thing—but Will Darrow sure wasn't one of them. He just didn't have the social graces for it.

But with Tess he hadn't felt any pressure to perform according to specific social standards, or to abide by any kind of vague, nebulous rules of dating. Because, hey, it was *Tess*. They hadn't been on a *date*. Even if it had...sort of...you know...felt like one.

Especially when it had come time for him to leave, and Tess had switched on the front porch light, because it was so late—after midnight, which he still couldn't get over—and had opened the door for Will to go, and Will had realized he hadn't wanted to go, certainly not before giving her a kiss good-night.

A kiss good-night, he recalled now. That had actually been what his instincts had told him to do: kiss her good-night. And not some sweet, brotherly peck on the cheek, either. No his instincts, damn them for the randy little buggers that they were, had told Will—no, had *commanded* him—to pull Tess into his arms and lay one on her that she wasn't likely to forget anytime soon.

She'd just looked so incredibly sexy in that little dress that showed off more skin than Will was used to seeing. Yeah, it had covered everything that needed covering and, yeah, it had been perfectly appropriate for a first-grade teacher. But it had also been so...so...so...

He sighed fitfully as he recalled her creamy shoulders and slender neck and the pale, silky flesh above her breasts and the barest hint of the faint, dusky valley between those breasts. And he thought now what he had thought then: *Oh, man.*

But Will had somehow mustered the fortitude to resist his instincts, and he hadn't kissed Tess good-night. He'd just done what he always did when faced with his strange, libidinous, lusty feelings for her. He'd reached out a hand toward her and then slowly, very slowly, he had…

…ruffled her hair.

He groaned now at the recollection. He knew she hated it when he did that, and frankly, he felt like a jerk whenever he performed the gesture. She wasn't a kid anymore; she was a grown woman. But what the hell was he supposed to have done? Kissed her? He couldn't do *that*.

Because it hadn't been a date, he reminded himself firmly again. It had just been dinner at the Monahan house, something Will had enjoyed a million times over during his life. It had come about because he and Tess had just so happened to be hungry in the same place at the same time. Dinner had been the next reasonable step.

Yeah, that was it, he thought now. He and Tess really hadn't had a date. What they'd had was a *logical conclusion,* that was all.

Of course, that didn't explain the paint cans and drop cloth and rollers and other painting accouterments that lay in the bed of Will's pickup truck right now. Because *painting the baby's room* wasn't exactly the next reasonable step to follow after dinner. And it wasn't a logical anything. Not for normal people, anyway.

Then again, Will hadn't much felt normal since the afternoon Abigail Torrance had blurted out that Tess Monahan was pregnant with another man's child, had he? Because there *was* nothing normal about Tess being pregnant with another man's child.

And dammit, why couldn't he stop thinking about the father of Tess's baby as *another man?*

Because you're not normal, that's why, Will told himself. *Anybody who was normal would be at work where he was supposed to be right now, and not headed in to paint a house without even having that house's occupant's permission.*

But he'd get permission before he painted. Of course he would. And, hey, it wasn't as if he'd already chosen the color and everything. He'd just brought white trim paint today, to get started on that. Okay, and some paint chips for Tess to look at, too. And, all right, so the majority of those paint chips were yellow in one of the color's many incarnations. Tess liked yellow. She wore a lot of yellow. She looked really pretty in yellow. Yellow was sorta generic, too, so a yellow nursery would be suitable for a baby of either gender. At least Will was offering her a choice of *which* yellow.

Though he rather liked the Moonstruck Gold himself. Then again, the Bright Papaya was kind of nice, too, if a little showy. But the Pale Buttercup would probably be best, under the circumstances. Still, he'd let Tess make the final decision. After pointing out how the Moonstruck Gold just caught the light so nicely.

He had unloaded the step ladder and was reaching for the drop cloth when Tess opened her front door and stepped out onto the porch. Immediately, Will felt vindicated, because she was wearing—*Ta da!*—yellow. That vindication turned into something else entirely, however, when he realized that the yellow garment in question was a bathing suit.

His first thought was that he really shouldn't be looking at Tess Monahan when she was wearing a bathing suit. His second thought was that he really shouldn't be getting this turned on by a bathing suit that looked like that.

Because really, when all was said and done, it was the most boring bathing suit Will had ever seen. One piece.

Wide shoulder straps. Low cut legs. High cut bodice. In other words, *everything* left to the imagination.

Which maybe, now that he thought more about it, was why his imagination was suddenly running wild. Because much to his dismay, he could imagine really well—and *was* imagining really well—what lay beneath that boring bathing suit. And what lay beneath that boring bathing suit was really, really exciting. Because what lay beneath that boring bathing suit was, well...Tess Monahan.

Oh, man.

Will squinched his eyes shut tight. *The capital of Nevada is Carson City,* he recited to himself. *The chemical abbreviation for common table salt is NaCl. The Seven Deadly Sins are Pride, Envy, Anger, Lust—*

Oops. Better try a different trivial pursuit.

But no matter how hard Will tried, he simply could not budge the image of Tess in her bathing suit from his brain. Which was just as well, because when he opened his eyes again, she was still standing there, framed by the front porch...dressed in her bathing suit. But just as he resigned himself to enjoying the sight of her standing there—well, hell, what else was he supposed to do?— she began to shrug into an oversize white shirt that fell to midthigh.

Oh, fine, he thought. Just when he was getting resigned, too. Then again, he pointed out to himself, heartening some, she hadn't buttoned the shirt up, had she?

But even that strange thought faded away, because Will realized it didn't matter if Tess put on a shirt or a raincoat or a suit of armor, for that matter. The sight of her in that bathing suit would be branded on his brain for time immemorial. Strangely, though, the recognition of the fact that he would carry the memory around with him forever made Will feel *not* uncomfortable, but kind of…sort of…good. In fact, he realized, much to his surprise, it made him feel *very* good.

"Hi," Tess called out from the porch as she descended the steps.

And, he noted with a barely suppressed groan of dissatisfaction, began to button her shirt from the bottom, up. A not-so-tiny part of him rejoiced, however, when she stopped at button number three. He watched her with not-so-lazy interest as she drew nearer, noting the subtle sway of her hips beneath the shirt, the pink polish on her toenails and the way the sunlight danced in her hair.

Nope, Tess was definitely not a kid anymore, he thought again. So why was he so frightened by his awareness of her, his desire for her? What was the problem with wanting her as much as he did? Well, aside from her being pregnant with another man's child, anyway. And aside from her just having a crush on him and nothing more. And aside from her big brother being his best friend, which would make for some unpleasantness if things between Will and Tess went sour. Not that they'd necessarily go sour.

Especially if they didn't go anywhere at all, he thought.

Okay, so he was starting to see now what the problem was with wanting her as much as he did. She had a definite tie to another man, by way of that little bun in her oven, a man who might still mean something to her, even if he was a former scumbag mobster. And any feelings Tess might have for Will were no doubt generated by some capricious crush she'd had on him since she was ten—which was by no means a guarantee that they'd turn into anything even remotely resembling a strong emotional commitment.

Not to mention the fact that Tess's older broth-

er...broth*ers,* he corrected himself—all *five* of them—
would pound Will into a greasy pulp if he ever did anything that might hurt her.

So that could be kind of a problem.

Gee, he'd just made the trip from upbeat to defeated
in six seconds flat, Will thought. That was a new record.

"What are you doing here?" Tess asked him pointedly
as she came to a halt before him.

He wished he could give her a pointed answer, too.
But the truth was he didn't honestly *know* what he was
doing here. Then he took one look at her face and he
remembered. Up close she looked even more bewitching
than she had from a distance. She looked more bothered
and more bewildered, too.

Maybe even as bothered and bewildered as Will was
himself. And that was saying something.

"Hi back atcha," he said, stalling. He retrieved the
ladder and leaned it against the side of the truck, then
wadded up the drop cloth and tossed it over one shoulder.
Then he glanced meaningfully down at his white
painter's pants and white V-neck T-shirt, both splattered
quite liberally with a spectrum's assortment of tints. "I'm
here to paint," he finally said—pointedly, too, he thought
proudly.

Her smile, which had been a bit uncertain to begin
with, fell some. "Paint what?" she asked.

As if she didn't know. Oh, she was just so cute when
she was teasing, Will thought wryly. "The baby's
room," he said. "Remember? I told you the other night
I'd come over and do it."

She shook her head. "No, you didn't. The other night
we both agreed that the room could use paint, but there
was never anything said about actually painting it."

Will grinned as he hefted up a paint can in one hand

and the step ladder in the other, then began to stride toward the house. "Well, I guess I stand corrected, then," he threw easily over his shoulder as he covered the short distance between driveway and porch, disposing of the four stairs in two effortless strides.

"Will!" Tess called after him.

But it took her a minute to realize how serious he was, and since he had the element of surprise on his side, he had already reached the top of the front stairwell inside the house before she caught up to him. When she did, she wrapped her fingers gently over his upper arm and spun him around with surprising strength. But she didn't let go of him when she completed the maneuver, only kept her fingers curved intimately over his bare flesh.

"What do you think you're doing?" she asked a little breathlessly.

In the moment when her fingers closed over his arm, Will realized three things simultaneously. One, the innocent gesture felt surprisingly intimate. Two, he still wanted, very badly, to kiss her. And three, the realization that he wanted to kiss her didn't frighten him nearly as much as it had before.

"Tess—" he began softly.

"You can't paint right now," she interrupted him— but she didn't let go of him.

And it was just as well that she'd interrupted him, he thought, seeing as how he didn't know what he was going to say to her, anyway. How could he possibly know what to say when he was feeling so suddenly—and so profoundly—confused?

"I was just leaving—I'm headed to the pool," she continued when he didn't respond. She still sounded a little breathless. She still didn't release him.

She still looked way too kissable.

''To meet some friends,'' she added, her focus on his face not quite as sharp as it had been before.

That was probably, Will thought, because her eyes were starting to look a little glazed, and because her gaze had dropped to his mouth. And when had she moved so close to him? he wondered, noting that her body was suddenly almost flush with his own. Or had *he* moved closer to *her?* And why was his heart hammering so hard in his chest? Why was his breathing beginning to feel so shallow? Hey, who turned out the lights…?

The next thing Will knew, he was brushing his lips lightly, gently, chastely over Tess's, and the entire world was crumbling away beneath his feet. Vaguely he registered the harmony of her sigh as it coupled with his, the sweetness of her breath as it mingled with his, the warmth of her presence as it joined with his.

And then, way, way off in the distance, he registered the cacophony of a step ladder crashing against the floor and a paint can thumping down the stairs. But he ignored the noise as he roped his arms around Tess's waist and pulled her more fully into his arms.

After that he registered nothing but physical sensation, responding to the irresistible feel of having her in his embrace and the eager way she returned his kiss. She wrapped her arms around his waist and pushed herself up on tiptoe to meet him, and at those enthusiastic gestures, he pulled her closer still.

He tangled one hand in her hair, weaving and sifting the silky tresses through his fingers as if it were spun gold, and thought he would die with wanting her. He cupped his palm over the crown of her head and turned it to the side to plunder her mouth more completely. And unable to help himself, he scooped a hand lower, dipped it beneath the hem of her shirt and curved his fingers capably—possessively—over the soft swell of her derriere. And nudging her gently forward, he pushed his pelvis enthusiastically against hers.

Whether her response to the action was a sigh or a gasp, Will never really decided. But she murmured something unintelligible against his lips, and he answered in kind, sweeping his tongue into her mouth to taste her as deeply as he could. And in that frenzied, incoherent moment, with that single, softly whispered response, he knew they had just generated something neither of them had anticipated.

He knew, too, that it was something neither of them would be able to escape. And he knew something else, as well. He knew that he had to have Tess, right then, right there, in the most basic, most intimate, most primitive way a man could join with a woman. And damn the consequences. He'd worry about the consequences later. Right now...

Oh, right now.

He intensified the kiss until Tess fisted both hands in his shirt and crowded her body completely into his. Her soft breasts crushed against his chest, and he gripped more firmly the taut flesh of her fanny cradled in his palm. Over and over he plundered her mouth with his, as she demanded more and more from him. He was lifting a hand to unfasten the bottom button on her shirt when the grating rasp of the doorbell below erupted like a drunken circus barker.

Then, ''Tessie!'' a male voice called out from below. ''You home?''

Tess sprang away from Will as if he had just caught on fire—which, he had to admit, was an all too fitting analogy. Reluctantly he let her go, mostly because he was too confused not to.

What the hell had just happened? he wondered as he scrubbed his hands over his face and through his hair. One minute he and Tess had been disagreeing over a paint job, and the next, they'd practically been making love right there at the top of the stairs. Just what the hell was going on?

He was almost afraid to look at her, and when he somehow found the fortitude to do just that, he wished he hadn't. Because Tess had spun completely around, had literally turned her back on him. She had also covered her face with both hands, and her shoulders were rising and falling rapidly with her ragged respiration.

"Tess?" he asked softly. "Are you okay?" He reached out to her, but something stayed his hand before he actually touched her. Reluctantly he let his arm fall back to his side. And when he did, something inside him went cold and empty.

She nodded slowly in response to his question, but said nothing. Nor did she turn around to look at him.

"Tessie!" the voice from below shouted up again. This time the summons was punctuated by the slamming of the screen door. "C'mon! I know you're home—I saw your car! I saw Will's truck out front, too! Where are you guys?"

Now that he paid closer attention, Will identified the voice as Sean Monahan's, and was only marginally relieved. At least it wasn't Finn, he tried to reassure himself. Finn, who would have known immediately that Will had just been groping his kid sister and who would have promptly fed him a knuckle sandwich or two—or ten— for doing so. Then again, Sean wasn't much better about that groping business. In spite of his easygoing disposition, the second oldest Monahan son could be pretty formidable, too, when he put his mind to it.

Fortunately, Sean was a lot more self-absorbed than Finn was, and for that reason he probably wouldn't have a clue as to what had just transpired between Will and Tess. Not unless he noticed how hard the two of them were breathing. Not unless he noticed the heat flooding Will's face and the stiff bulge surging against his fly. Not unless Sean noticed how pink-cheeked Tess was, too, Will thought further when she finally turned around. Not unless he noticed the tears in her eyes.

Whoa, hold on. Back up. Tears? Tess was crying?

Before he could ask her about it, she swiped her hands fiercely over her face, wiping the dampness away. And none too soon, either, because that was when Sean Monahan stepped out of the living room and paused at the foot of the steps below them.

"What's up?" he asked the couple, sounding only mildly suspicious.

Will squeezed his eyes shut tight at the phrasing. *You do not want to know,* he thought, recalling that surging-bulge business.

Oh, boy, were things complicated now.

Seven

Tess flinched at hearing Sean's question. If he only knew how easily misconstrued the simple query could be. Because there was *a lot* up in the Monahan house at the moment. Her temperature for one. Her heart rate for another. Her libido for a third. And she wasn't *even* going to begin listing all the things that were *up* with—and on—Will.

Uh-uh. No way. No how.

So instead of answering Sean's question—how could she, when she had completely misplaced her voice, not to mention her reason and sanity?—she inhaled another deep breath and tried in vain to focus her attention, among other things, on the matter at hand. And she wondered vaguely when the asteroid that was currently hurtling her through space was going to slow down. Because that could be the only explanation for why she felt so breathless, so weightless, so utterly nebulous at the moment.

What on earth had just happened? she wondered wildly. To her right stood a man she had loved since she was old enough to understand what loving was, a man who, until a few moments ago, had never offered her a more familiar touch than to ruffle her hair. *Ruffle her hair.* One minute he'd been talking to her as if she were still a twelve-year-old girl, and he knew what was best for her. And then the next minute, he'd been rubbing his body hotly against hers and touching parts of her she'd scarcely touched herself.

Oh, yeah, she thought. He definitely did know what was best for her. But just when she'd begun to enjoy it, just when she was experiencing a veritable explosion of newfound sensation and possibility with the man in question, her brother had to come along and turn a fire hose on everything. And just like that, her sexual awakening, one that had literally brought her to tears, had been fully and completely sedated.

How ironic, Tess thought, that it had been Sean—who had never put the brakes on *any* relationship *he'd* ever had—who had been the one to do it.

The Monahan brother in question stood at the foot of the stairs now, hands fisted on his denim-clad hips, gazing up at the still-unresponsive couple with *much* curiosity. "Hel-lo-o-o?" he called up to them. His blue eyes danced with laughter, but that was nothing new. Sean never took anything seriously. "Anybody home?" he asked meaningfully. "Physically *or* mentally? I'll take either."

"Hi, Sean."

Surprisingly, it was Will, and not Tess, who answered the question. Or maybe that wasn't so surprising, she thought, seeing as how her voice was still lodged somewhere between her diaphragm and the planet Pluto.

"Painting today, are we?" Sean asked, nodding first at Will's attire, then at the paint can that lay on its side at his feet. "Though that's going to be kind of tough with you up there and the paint down here. Just what *are* you painting, anyway, the pool?" he asked further, this time indicating Tess's swimsuit. "Funny, I don't remember this house having a pool."

"Will's going to paint the baby's room," Tess piped up without thinking.

Immediately she squeezed her eyes shut tight. She really was beginning to wonder about her own sanity. Then again, the paint *was* for the baby's room, she reminded herself. There just wasn't any *baby* for the baby's room, that was all.

"I mean..." she tried again. Then she halted herself. Why bother? she thought. Sean had bought into the gossip, too.

"Will is painting the baby's room?" her brother echoed, arching his dark eyebrows in surprise. "Why?"

"Because none of you mooks offered to do it," Will piped up before Tess could reply. "That's why."

Sean nodded, crossing his arms over the red T-shirt stretched taut across his chest. "Yeah, and I heard about the baby's father being in the Witness Protection Program, so unless he's got one of those extralong mop handles for the roller, he's not going to be any help at all, is he?"

Tess rolled her eyes. Great. She should have known that story would have circulated back to her brothers by now. At this point everyone in town probably knew about her imaginary baby's connection to the mob. The Marigold Craft Circle was probably knitting her a little pair of handcuffs right about now. The cake at her baby shower would no doubt have a file baked into it. She would have to name the child Vito or Angela.

In a last-ditch effort to defend her nonexistent baby's nonexistent heritage—but still remain honest in the process—she said, "Sean, there is no—"

Her brother held up his hands, palm out, and interrupted her, "Yeah, yeah, yeah. I know. There is no reason to criticize the baby's father. He's not bad. He's just misunderstood, right?"

Tess shook her head. "No, he's—"

"I mean, he must have had *some* decent quality," Sean continued, oblivious to her objection, "because you're too smart a girl to fall for some lowlife crook. But, Tess, come on. The mob? What were you thinking?"

"I—"

"She *wasn't* thinking," Will said in her defense. Sort of. "She was in love with the guy. Weren't you, Tess?" When he turned to her for confirmation, she could have sworn Will looked hurt. "And love makes people do crazy stuff."

It does? Tess wondered, feeling strangely warm and fuzzy inside for some reason. "Actually, I—" she began.

"So lay off, Sean." Will went back to berating her brother before she could quite get the words out. "Quit giving her a hard time. Like you've never made a mistake over a woman before."

"Actually, no. I haven't," Sean replied smugly. "But then, women just naturally adore me," he added in as matter-of-fact a voice as Tess had ever heard. "And it's hard to make a mistake with a woman under those circumstances. But you're right. Tess is different in that respect. I'm sure she did at least *think* she was in love with the baby's father."

"I wasn't in love with him," she finally managed to get in.

Both men whipped their attention back to her face, and she realized she'd just unwittingly reintroduced that one-night-stand thing. "I mean...uh..."

"Don't try to explain, Tess," Sean said. "Just know that we're here for you. And if the baby's father does come around...?" He doubled one fist and smacked it—hard—against his other open palm. "The Monahan boys will be waiting to have a little chat with him."

Oh, boy.

"Is that why you came over?" she asked wearily. "To threaten the baby's father?"

Sean shook his head. "That wasn't the only reason, no."

"Then what?"

"I need to get a couple of Dad's tools out of the garage."

Tess waved him off in that general direction. "Fine. Help yourself."

But instead of following her instructions, Sean turned to Will. "You want a hand with the painting?" he asked. "I'm not working on anything that can't wait a couple days."

Silently Tess willed *both* men to go away, to leave her alone so that she could explore this strange new development in her nonrelationship with Will. Unfortunately, being men, they didn't pick up on her feminine mystique at all.

"Sure," Will agreed readily. "With two of us, we can trim the room out in one afternoon."

Sean leaned down to pick up the wayward paint can. "Sounds good," he said as he made his way up the stairs.

Good, she echoed to herself as he pushed past her.

Right. That was the last word she'd use to describe the
situation. Especially when, with one final, longing look
her way, Will snatched up the step ladder and followed
him.

With Sean and Will working together, the two men
completed their work in record time. It was an afternoon
well spent, as far as Will was concerned. There was nothing like completing a job, and doing it well, to leave a
man feeling, well...manly.

On the downside, though, having the work finished
meant that Sean had no reason to hang around and so
left at just after five o'clock. And after that Will was
faced with the same dilemma he had faced two nights
before: he was hungry and in the same vicinity as Tess.
Which meant it was time for another one of those logical
conclusions—dinner.

Except this time things would more than likely end
differently from how they had ended last time. Because
tonight, when Will's instincts commanded him to kiss
Tess good-night, he was fairly certain he wouldn't be
able to ignore them. In fact, he'd probably completely
override them and go way beyond a simple good-night
buss.

He still couldn't imagine what had come over him earlier that afternoon to make him kiss Tess the way he had.
Kiss. Hell. What he'd done had gone way beyond kissing.
Consuming might be a more appropriate way to describe
what he had attempted to do to her. *Possessing* might be
another. Or even *sharing of souls*—not to mention *body
parts*.

Whatever it had been, it had been damned pleasant.
He just wished he could come up with some explanation
as to *why* it had happened.

Tess had just looked so... And the way she had been gazing at him had just been so... And the way he had started to feel had just been so... And something in the air had just demanded that he... And then, the next thing he knew the two of them had just been...

He sighed heavily as he capped the paint can and collected an assortment of brushes for cleaning. Obviously, he couldn't form an adequate answer to any of the questions that were tumbling around in his head. Probably because he couldn't quite *complete* any of the questions that were tumbling around in his head.

Obviously, he didn't know when or how or why things had changed between him and Tess. Obviously, he had no idea what had caused him to do what he had done. Obviously, there was no way he could explain why she had responded to him as eagerly as she had. In fact, there was only *one* thing Will *could* say obviously for sure.

He wanted to do it all again. Real soon, too.

Especially when he made his way down to the kitchen and found Tess standing there, pondering the contents of her pantry as if they held the answers to the mysteries of the universe. She looked cool and crisp—and kissable, dammit—in a wispy, gauzy dress the color of ripe celery, and all Will could do was think again about how good it had felt to hold her.

She had vacated the premises that afternoon, shortly after Sean's arrival, had gone to meet her friends at the pool as planned. And she'd returned home while Will was in the kitchen getting a drink of water, her wet hair pushed back from her forehead, her damp swimsuit clinging to her even more suggestively than it had before, her shirt tied carelessly around her waist.

It had been all he could do not to wrestle her to the floor right there and consummate whatever this wild, wanton thing was between them. Had it not been for Sean upstairs, shouting down for Will to bring him a glass of water, too, he probably would have done just that.

But Sean wasn't here now. Will and Tess were alone. There was nothing to stop them from picking up right where they'd left off earlier. Well, nothing physical at any rate. Emotionally, however, things still felt a little shaky.

Oh, who was he kidding? he demanded of himself. Emotionally, things still felt *very* shaky.

"Hi," Tess said softly when she saw him. She pushed the pantry door closed and turned to face him. "Did you guys finish the trimming?"

Will nodded and made his way toward the sink, trying very, very hard not to brush up against Tess—or reach out for her or look at her or smell her or acknowledge her in any way—as he went. "Yeah," he told her, "we finished."

But the trim job he'd just completed was the last thing on Will's mind at the moment. Instead, he was wondering how he was going to broach the subject of what had happened on the stairwell landing a little while ago. Because there was no way he would be leaving this house until the two of them had a few things settled. He wasn't going anywhere until he understood just what exactly had erupted between the two of them.

Yeah, he'd been having lusty thoughts about Tess for the past few years now. Yeah, he knew she'd had a crush on him for a long, long time. Yeah, it made sense that two grown adults who were as aware of each other as he and Tess obviously were would, when they were left alone, eventually be driven to act on that attraction. But their embrace had gone way beyond a curious, let's-see-what-happens exploration. It had been a flat-out explosion of need. At least, it had been for Will. He still wasn't sure if Tess's response had been as extreme as his own.

Sure had felt like it, though.

He opened his mouth to initiate just such a dialogue with her, but, much to his surprise, the question that came out was, "Did you get a chance to look at those paint chips I brought, and pick out a color for the walls?"

She moved to the kitchen table and glanced down at the array of multitinted cards scattered there. "Gee, here's a radical thought," she said mildly as she sorted through them, "how about yellow?"

"Good choice," he told her as he adjusted the temperature of the water to a nice warm degree and thrust the paint brushes under the stream. "I liked yellow the best, myself."

"Wow, what an amazing coincidence," she said blandly. "How could I have possibly guessed that? I mean, the percentage of yellow shades here is only, what? Ninety-eight percent?"

He shrugged, smiling. "I know you like yellow."

"How do you know that?"

He shrugged again, a bit less successfully this time. "You wear yellow a lot."

There was a small, meaningful silence on her part, followed by a softly uttered, "You notice what I wear?"

He gave up the pretense of cleaning paintbrushes, turned off the water and wiped his hands on a paper towel. Then he spun around to gaze at her fully. "I notice a lot, Tess. More than you think."

Her lips parted fractionally in surprise, but she said nothing that would give him a clue as to what she might really be thinking. So, feeling reckless, he continued. "For instance, I noticed how much you responded to me earlier, when I...kissed you."

That finally broke the ice. "*You* kissed *me?*" she asked, faintly incredulous. "Here, all afternoon, I've been wondering how I was going to explain the fact that *I* kissed *you.*" She smiled a bit nervously. "I guess I still have a lot to learn about—"

She stopped right there, as if she were afraid of revealing too much. But Will wasn't about to let her off that easily. "Seems to me you know everything you need to know about it," he told her.

At no time had he meant to give the statement any kind of double-edged significance. He'd only meant to tell her that she had been really, really good at kissing him, because no woman had made him feel the way Tess had made him feel in those few brief moments the two of them had been entwined. But she must have taken his remark the wrong way, because she blushed furiously, her lips tightened into a flat line, and she narrowed her eyes almost menacingly.

"Why do you say that?" she demanded coolly. "You think I must know everything because I'm pregnant? Because I've slept around? Because I'm easy? Is that what you mean?"

"Oh, Tess." He shook his head. "That wasn't what I meant at all. I would never think any of those things about you."

In three easy strides, each covered more quickly than the one before, he crossed to where she was standing. Gently he cupped his arms over her bare shoulders and tried not to notice how soft, how warm, how silky was the skin beneath his fingertips. Tried...and failed miserably. Because the moment he touched Tess, Will registered every glorious detail about her. And it only made him want to know more.

"I only meant," he said, "that you don't have anything to learn, because you made me feel so...so good. So right. It feels good to hold you, Tess. To touch you. To kiss...''

Words failed him after that, but that was okay, because none really seemed necessary. The same odd spell that had fallen over him that afternoon quickly overtook him again. He almost felt as if there were someone else acting on his behalf when he pulled Tess forward, dipped his head to hers and covered her mouth with his. But the moment his lips made contact with hers, he knew it wasn't someone else acting. Because a heat and a desire and a need uncoiled inside him that he couldn't possibly deny. And he knew then that what was happening was happening to him.

And he knew it was happening to Tess, too, because she immediately looped her arms around his waist and pushed herself closer, upward, to receive more fully his kiss. And, he quickly realized, much to his delight, to kiss him back. Because there was no arguing that she quickly took the initiative, that she was indeed the one kissing Will this time.

So what else could he do but let her?

Tess pushed herself higher and nearer to Will and reveled in the way he settled his arms around her waist as if it were the most natural gesture in the world. She couldn't imagine what had come over her to make her behave so boldly, so brazenly, but at the moment she didn't much care. She simply hadn't been able to tolerate the thought of letting this opportunity slip away, the way the last one had. She wanted—needed—to explore more fully this strange, spontaneous thing that had exploded between them that afternoon. She needed a chance to investigate precisely what it was that had propelled them together this way.

Tess had practically lived her life for a chance to have Will Darrow in her arms. One kiss, she'd always told herself. If she could just give him one kiss, she could make him understand how very much she loved him. And with one kiss, she'd always been certain, she could make Will love her back.

Earlier that day, before Sean had interrupted them, she'd been so sure that she and Will were destined for that ultimate union between a man and a woman. The way he had held her, the way he had touched her, the way he had kissed her, had all indicated in no uncertain terms what would be happening next. Had Sean not shown up, Will and Tess would have ended up in her bed; she was sure of it.

And she had been ready for it. She'd been ready for it then, and she was ready for it now. In some ways it was what she had been planning for since she was a teenager, capable of understanding the physical mechanics of sex. She'd wanted Will for what felt like a lifetime. And now...

Now she was going to have him.

The realization of that set a match to Tess's passion, kindling it, inflaming it, until she felt as if she would catch fire. Then she felt Will's fingers cupping snugly around her waist, scooting higher up her rib cage, and she did catch fire. His other hand quickly followed suit, his fingers curling possessively into her sensitive flesh, and she cursed the delicate fabric of her dress for its very existence.

His mouth on hers pressed harder, as if he were trying to usurp control from her. But she wasn't willing to give him that just yet. So she scooted her hands up over his torso, fingering every solid ridge of muscle and cord of sinew as she went. He was hot hammered steel beneath her fingertips, even with the fabric of his shirt hindering her study. Soon, she told herself. Soon she would run her hands over every naked inch of him. For now, though, she only linked her fingers behind his neck and pulled him down to intensify their kiss.

He growled something incoherent against her lips, but complied with her command, bending his body at the waist to better accommodate her. Tess drove her fingers into the silky hair she encountered above his nape, loving the way it felt as it sifted and scythed over her skin. His mouth was supple and strong against hers, warm and damp and inviting. Experimentally she touched the tip of her tongue to his lower lip, and the hands that had been skimming up and down her rib cage came to an abrupt halt. She was about to apologize for whatever she had done when Will suddenly wrapped his arms completely around her back and jerked her close.

Oh. Okay. So that tongue on the lip thing must be something he liked.

She formed the observation vaguely, then touched her tongue to his lower lip again. This time, though, she dragged it slowly over the plump arc of his lip, from one side to the other and back again. Will remained utterly still, save the rapid-fire rush of his breath mingling with the shuddering quickness of her own. He tasted so good. Like salt and man and something else she couldn't quite identify.

The hands splayed open on her back pushed her forward, until Tess's body was completely flush with Will's. And then she felt the hammering of his heart against his rib cage, mimicking almost exactly the ragged, rampant pulsing of her own. She kissed him more deeply, sweeping her tongue delicately into his mouth in a manner that was completely instinctive. She'd never kissed a man in such a way before. Had never wanted to. With Will, though, she wanted to join as much of herself to him as she could.

But the moment she filled his mouth, the balance of power shifted, and Will easily assumed control. He sucked her tongue deeper inside, locking it with his own, then straightened, pulling her up with him. Tess's feet actually left the floor as he roped his arms around her waist and pulled her higher, and she looped her own arms around his neck to anchor herself to him. But instead of holding her there, Will set her down on the kitchen counter, maneuvering himself between her legs. He settled his hands lightly on her waist and kissed her again, with a bit less fierceness this time.

Then, "Tess," he ground out as he tore his mouth away from hers. He inhaled a few irregular breaths, then plunged on, "I don't know what's happening here, and even though I know the smart thing to do—probably—would be to put the brakes on it, I don't want to stop."

She met his gaze levelly, thinking his blue eyes seemed darker somehow, deeper, more expressive than ever before. "I don't want to stop, either," she assured him.

"But I know you're in a rough spot right now, with everything that's going on," he continued. "Your life is in a jumble. I don't want to confuse you any more than you already are. I know you must still have feelings for the baby's father, and—"

"There's no one else, Will," she vowed solemnly. She lifted a hand to thread her fingers through the soft hair at his temple. To herself, she added silently, *There's never been anyone else. No one but you. It was always you.*

She told herself to say the words out loud, to let him know how very important he was, to emphasize how momentous this occasion was going to be for her. But she couldn't quite bring herself to put voice to her feelings. She knew she loved Will, and she knew that he cared for her. Maybe, someday, his affection would turn to love. Right now Tess didn't want to think about that. So she focused on how much she wanted Will. And on how much he obviously wanted her. There was nothing to stop them from doing what each clearly wanted to do. And Tess was ready.

"But the baby's father," Will objected.

"There is no one else," she repeated, more adamantly this time.

For a moment she thought he would reconsider their position, would withdraw from her completely. Instead, his gaze still fixed intently on hers, he skimmed his hands downward, over the flair of her hips, down her thighs, along her calves, until he came to the hem of her dress. She wasn't wearing shoes or stockings, and the moment she felt his fingertips grazing over her bare flesh, the significance of what they were going to do washed fully over her.

But she had no misgivings, not a single second thought. All Tess wanted was right here. Because all she wanted now was what she had wanted all along.

All Tess wanted was Will.

Eight

He must have understood that somehow, because just as she settled her hands on his strong shoulders, he began to slowly, slowly, oh, so slowly push her dress up over her legs. Little by little the warm summer air replaced the gauzy fabric, until it was bunched around her thighs, halted by her sitting position. That didn't stop Will, however, from dipping his hands beneath the garment to continue on his journey.

The brush of his warm, rough fingertips gliding over her bare thighs was such sweet torture. Heat puddled in her midsection, growing hotter with each pass of his hand, until it began to spread in languid circles through her entire body. Will cupped his fingers over her legs and brushed the pads of his thumbs indolently up and down the sensitive skin of her inner thighs. Tess watched as his eyes went darker, as his cheeks grew flushed, as his lips parted fractionally, as if he weren't quite getting enough air. His was the expression of a man overcome by his passion, and she could scarcely believe she had been the one to rouse it.

Involuntarily she closed her eyes, and in doing so, registered the gentle brush of his fingers even more keenly. Instinctively she opened her legs wider and felt Will move more resolutely between them. When he dipped his head to her neck and dragged his open mouth along the tender column of her throat, she tangled her fingers in his hair and murmured his name. The hands on her thighs moved higher...higher...higher still, until they reached the edge of her panties.

But that delicate barrier proved no hindrance to Will. He simply tucked his fingers beneath the lacy openings, moving one hand to the curve of her bottom, the other to the nest of curls between her legs. Tess cried out at the twin touches, gasping to recall the breath that shot from her lungs. Will's thumb furrowed purposely through the damp folds of her skin until he located the ultrasensitive bud nestled there. Then, with one exquisite touch, he brought Tess to near-delirium.

Never in her life had she felt anything like the hot rush of awareness that raced through her as he fondled her. Her hands stilled in his hair, and her entire body went limp as he stroked her, again and again and again. She sensed him pulling back from her, watching her reaction. But she didn't dare open her eyes, fearing her barely banked response would explode right there.

"Oh, God, you are so sexy" she heard him murmur.

Then, before she even realized his intention, he scooped her off the counter and into his arms.

She cried out her objection at his abandonment, but Will ignored it. The next thing Tess knew, he was carrying her up the stairs, down the hall, to her bedroom.

He didn't bother to close the door, only set her down gently at the center of her bed. He said not a word as he reached behind himself to bunch his T-shirt in one fist and jerk it over his head. Then he discarded it and sat down on the bed to tug off his shoes. Those, too, he hastily kicked away, then he stood and went to work on his pants.

Tess found it impossible to look away from him. He was so glorious, his chest and torso ridged with muscle and dusted liberally with dark hair. She'd seen him without a shirt before, on many occasions. But not like this. Never like this. Because for the first time she would be able to touch him, really touch him, the way she had only dreamed of touching him before.

When he stepped out of his pants and tossed them to the floor near his shirt, she couldn't help but glance away. She felt suddenly and inordinately modest, despite the intimate touches he had just shared with her. As he shed the last of his clothing, Tess started to rise from the bed, to remove hers, as well. But modesty overcame her again, and for the first time she began to have second thoughts about what she and Will were going to do.

"Don't," he said softly.

Thinking he had read her thoughts, she turned to face him, then felt herself blush at the sight of him standing there, completely naked. She had thought his upper body was impressive, but it hadn't begun to prepare her for his lower half. To put it succinctly, Will was...he was...

Well, he *wasn't* succinct.

"Don't?" she echoed, forcing her gaze back up to his face.

"Don't get undressed," he clarified. "Let me do it."

Oh, my.

Another wave of heat splashed through her as she

watched him stride toward her. Without hesitation he settled his hands on her hips and bunched the loose fabric
in both fists. Then slowly he drew the garment up her
body, and the shiver of gauze felt like a match being
dragged over her heated, sensitive flesh. Will pulled the
dress over her head and tossed it to the floor, near where
his own clothes lay. Then he took another step forward
and reached behind her, for the clasp of her brassiere.

With one deft flick that garment, too, was gone, and,
instinctively, Tess lifted her arms to cover herself. Will
intercepted her, however, circling his fingers around each
wrist, pulling her arms open wide.

"Don't hide yourself," he said. "You're too beautiful
for hiding."

Tess felt herself coloring from head to toe when she
saw the expression on his face, one of total need and
unhampered desire. Experimentally he released one of
her wrists, and somehow she kept herself from crossing
it over her naked breasts. Instead Will opened his palm
over one, filling his hand with her, palming the distended
peak before releasing her other wrist to mimic the gesture
on her other breast.

"Oh," she whispered softly, the quiet sound all she
was able to manage in response to his caress. Again her
eyes fluttered shut at the sweep of pleasure that wound
through her at his touch.

She wanted to touch him, too, wanted to feel him
stretched out alongside her, so that every inch of his body
was pressing against hers. Slowly she backed up, step by
step, until her progress was hindered by the bed. Will
dropped his hands from her breasts to hook his fingers in
the waistband of her panties, then knelt to pull them
down over her thighs and calves.

Tess stepped out of them, then turned to pull the spread

and sheets down from the mattress. When she did, Will stepped behind her, spooning himself against her back. She felt his heavy member rubbing against the elegant cleft of her bottom, felt the softly coiling hair on his chest skimming over her bare back. He moved his hands forward again, covering her breasts, then dipped his head to kiss her neck and shoulders.

A wild heat shot through her again, and she spun around to cover his mouth with hers. As she kissed him, long and hard and deep, she sat down on the bed, pulling Will along with her. He came down over her, atop her, folding his arms to brace his elbows on the mattress, one on each side of her head. Again and again he plundered her mouth, tasting her to what felt like the depths of her soul.

Tess reached down between their bodies, searching until she found that part of his body that so intrigued her. Curling her fingers around his stiff shaft, she weighed the long length of him in her hand. Jerking his mouth from hers, Will threw back his head, sucking in a harsh breath at the contact.

Again and again, she moved her fingers along the rigid column, already made damp by his body's reaction to her touch. Over and over, she palmed the swollen head. Her gaze shifted to his as she continued to stroke him, and she saw that he had closed his eyes tight. She'd had no idea she could wield such power over a man. But Will was clearly in her thrall.

"I want you inside me," she said softly, thickly, as she drew her fingers along him again. "Deep inside me. I want to know what it's like to have you there."

Will opened his eyes at her roughly uttered declaration, and Tess caught her breath at what she beheld burning there. His pupils had expanded until she could scarcely see the blue, and fire—raging wildfire—burned in their limitless depths. His dark hair hung in wet, lank strands over his forehead, his lips were parted slightly, his cheeks were stained with the depth of his passion for her.

"You want me inside you?" he rasped out hoarsely in a voice she scarcely recognized as his.

Unable to utter a single sound in response, Tess only nodded slowly, silently.

"Then take me, Tess. I'm yours."

Instinct alone drove her as she bent her knees and opened her legs, then led him to where she was alive with need. He ducked his head to watch her actions, and Tess followed suit. Taking him in both her hands, she scooted her hips forward, upward. When she began to arch toward him, Will snatched one of the pillows from the head of the bed and thrust it beneath her hips. Then she positioned him at the damp opening of her desire and guided him inside.

Oh, the sensation that shot through her in feeling that initial contact. She'd never felt anything like it. The head of his shaft slipped deftly between the delicate folds of her flesh, and he rubbed himself in and out and along those moist furrows, readying himself to penetrate her more thoroughly. When he was slick with her passion, he pushed his body closer to hers and gently entered her tender canal. Tess braced herself for what she had heard might be painful, but all she felt for those first few moments was a gentle friction of motion as Will gradually moved deeper inside.

And then, suddenly, without warning, he shoved himself deeper still, completely inside her. Tess gasped at the keenness of the pain that knifed through her as he completed his thrust, in the process breaking through the barrier that no man had breached before. But the anguished sound she expelled was completely overshadowed by the cry of shock that thundered from Will when he realized what the breaching of that barrier signified. His entire body went still, and the hands on each side of her head fisted tight. When his eyes met hers, she saw fear and panic replacing the fire that had burned so brightly there. And something else, too...she wasn't quite sure what.

She could scarcely breathe, so frantic was the pain that sliced through her from pelvis to chest. Never had she imagined it would be like this. Never had she thought that her body would betray her this way. But she was so small and completely untried. And Will was so...

Oh.

She would never be the same again.

"Tess," he said, the roughness of his voice making her name sound like a foreign word. "Why didn't you *tell* me?"

She swallowed hard and tried fruitlessly to steady her breathing. In halting, gasping words, she assured him, "I...didn't...tell you...'cause it...it's not...important."

"Not important?" he echoed incredulously. "This is your first time, and you say it's not important?"

"Oh, that's...important," she whispered weakly. The pain was beginning to lessen some now. "And the fact that it's...that it's you...here with me...that's important. But nothing else, Will. Nothing else is...important. Just you. Only you." She hesitated only a moment before adding, very quietly, "I love you."

He'd squeezed his eyes shut tight before she got to those final three words, so she never really knew how he reacted to hearing them—or if he even heard them at all. By the time he opened his eyes again, they were clear and blue and...shuttered. At seeing his closed expression, another pain shot through Tess that had nothing to do with his invasion of her body.

"Am I hurting you?" he asked. But immediately he answered his own question. "What am I saying? Of course I'm hurting you."

He began to withdraw, so Tess wrapped her legs around his waist and her arms around his shoulders and held him where he was. "No," she said. "Don't stop. I want you, Will. I want you to make love to me."

He hesitated, clearly ambivalent. Tess decided to take it as a good sign. "Not if it's going to hurt you," he said softly.

"The worst of it is over," she told him. She didn't know if that were true or not, but she honestly didn't care. Despite the brief pain, being joined with Will felt good beyond her wildest expectations. "Please. Make love to me," she said. When he offered no response to her plea, one way or the other, she reiterated, more softly, more insistently, "Please, Will. Please."

Without a word, very, very slowly, and very, very gently, he began to pull his body out of hers. Tess was about to object again, more vehemently this time, when instead of leaving her, he braced his arms more resolutely on the mattress and pushed himself forward—more tenderly—again. The pain eased some this time as her body altered itself to better accommodate him. But he still filled her to capacity...and to the very depths of her soul.

She really wouldn't ever be the same.

She relaxed her legs, but didn't unwrap them from around his waist, and she clung to him as he slowly, gently, moved his body in and out of hers. With each new stroke, Tess felt herself changing, physically and emotionally, until the union of their bodies felt sure and natural and right. Once the pain subsided, the passion returned, and where there had been worry was joy.

Will, too, seemed to forget about the shock of what had happened, because he dropped his head to her breast and drew one nipple full into his mouth, laving it with the flat of his tongue before sucking harder. He fairly consumed her as he continued to glide in and out of her, and the twin sensations sent Tess's responses into overdrive.

A bubble of heat and ecstasy and something else she'd never felt before effervesced inside her, growing larger and more volatile with every passing second. With each new movement of Will's body against hers, and with each motion of her own in response, that bubble rose higher and higher, nearer the surface, filling Tess in a way she had never been filled before. Then, just when she thought she would go careering over the edge alone, Will's movements became more fretful, more urgent, more demanding. And she knew he was right there with her when the bubble exploded in a white-hot kaleidoscope of pleasure.

She'd never felt anything like it before. She clung to Will, gripping his strong shoulders with feverish fingers, pushing her body up to his for one final, earthy thrust. Something hot and wild rushed into her, through her, down to the very essence of her being. Will, she realized. Both physically and spiritually, he was in her now. He was *in* her.

And she knew that no matter what happened, that was where he would always remain.

Will awoke in Tess's bed a little before dawn the following morning. He could see beyond the lace curtains, fluttering silently in the damp, almost cool, early-morning breeze, that light would be upon them soon. Robins and wrens were twittering in the trees, and the faint sound of a distant train told him some people were already up and about and performing their jobs.

He should be up and about and performing his job, too, he thought. He liked to open the garage early, so people could stop in on their way to work or to run errands. But the soft, fragrant body nestled so snugly against his own prohibited him from moving, prohibited him from planning, prohibited him from thinking. Tess sighed in her sleep, unconsciously pushed herself more intimately against him, and Will realized how much he wanted her again.

Three things occurred to him at once. Number one, Tess was—or at least had been, until last night—a virgin. Number two, that meant she had been telling the truth all along and wasn't pregnant with someone else's child. And number three, she might very well be pregnant now—with Will's child.

Because in thinking that she was already pregnant, he hadn't bothered to use any kind of protection last night. And Tess, probably because it had been her first time and because she'd had her thoughts on other things—or, at the very least, on *one* other thing—hadn't used any, either.

In a word, oops.

Three things occurred to him at once. Number one, he'd just spent the night deflowering the kid sister of his best friend. Number two, he might just become a father in nine months' time, thanks to that deflowering. And number three, his best friend was now his former best friend, because Finn would doubtless beat the hell out of Will once he found out what had happened.

Nobody knocked up and abandoned Tess Monahan

and got away with it—not unless they went into the Witness Protection Program. And as good as the Witness Protection Program was beginning to look at the moment, Will knew it wasn't really a viable option.

Okay, so maybe, inadvertently, he had just created one huge problem where there hadn't been a single thing wrong before. He could fix this. He could. All he had to do was...

Marry Tess.

Marry Tess? he echoed incredulously to himself. Why did that, of all other solutions there might possibly be, pop into his head first and foremost? That was a bit drastic, wasn't it? Surely there was some other way to handle this. There was no guarantee that Tess was, in fact, pregnant. And nobody had to know that the two of them had just spent the night together. Making love. Three times. Even though that third time hadn't exactly included...you know...because Tess had been too tender. So they'd had to be inventive—really inventive, he recalled with a salacious grin—in bringing each other to fulfillment.

But nobody had to know that, he repeated to himself emphatically, stowing the erotic memories for now. Not unless...you know...Tess turned up pregnant. Nevertheless Will told himself not to overreact.

But what if she *was* pregnant? he asked himself. She'd already had to endure weeks of talk and speculation in Marigold about an illicit love affair and an illegitimate child, neither of which had ever even existed. Granted, that talk hadn't been malicious, but it hadn't exactly been beneficial to Tess, either.

Plus, she was just about to reach a point where she might finally prove to everyone that all the talk had been all talk. Because she was arriving at a point in her non-existent pregnancy where she would have started to show, had she actually been pregnant. And when she didn't, people would have no choice but to accept the fact that she wasn't going to have a baby, that the rabid rumor had been just that—a rabid *rumor*. Soon enough Tess would have been exonerated, vindicated, exculpated. But now...

Now, thanks to Will, she might be pregnant for real. And now, the father wasn't some fly-by-night deadbeat who'd committed crimes and been forced to abandon her. No, this time the father would be as real as the child. This time the father would be Will Darrow. And then the talk in town about illicit affairs and illegitimate children would be twice as fierce—not to mention accurate. Unless, of course, the two of them made everything licit and legitimate.

Marry Tess.

Oddly, the idea didn't bother Will nearly as much as he had thought it would, even though marriage was something he'd never realistically considered. He'd never had cause to explore the possibilities of tying his life to someone else's forever and ever, till death do them part. There had just never been anyone in his life he'd cared that much about. No one he could envision himself spending that much time with, without that time becoming tedious or predictable or routine. Simply put, he hadn't met the right person.

But now that he thought about marriage to Tess, he realized it might not be such a bad thing at that. They'd known each other since they were kids, they shared a similar heritage, a similar background, similar values. They had a lot in common personally. And they might very well have just created a baby together—Will couldn't conceive of a more unifying bond than that.

So they didn't have a be-all, end-all love to transcend

time. So what? Will wasn't convinced such an emotion even existed, anyway. Hey, there were worse reasons to get married than that you liked each other and were about to become parents. It could work.

Will was still mulling over this brave, new world of marital undertaking when he felt Tess stirring beside him. He didn't move himself, hoping she might go back to sleep and give him a few more precious moments to ponder the tumble of thoughts and emotions whirling like a twister inside him. Bit by bit, though, she awakened, uttering soft little sounds that were erotic as hell, rubbing her body with unconscious seductiveness along his. She curled her fingers gently into the dark hair on his chest, nuzzled his neck and brushed her lips lightly over the hollow at the base of his throat.

Then her eyes fluttered open, and, as consciousness finally dawned, she pushed herself away from him a bit. She reached up to nudge a handful of hair out of her eyes, met his gaze levelly and went absolutely still.

For a moment she seemed not to realize where she was, seemed not to remember what had happened the night before. In the semidarkness she seemed almost other-worldly, with her fair hair and ivory skin and eyes the color of the sky. Will held his breath to see how she would react, to see if she would burst into tears or run screaming from the room when she recalled what had happened the night before.

But all she did was smile a little sleepily, drop her hand back to his chest and murmur a soft "Good morning." Then she tugged the sheet up around her shoulders, looped her arms around his waist, and snuggled close to Will again.

He breathed a silent sigh of relief and was helpless to stop the smile that curled his lips. "Good morning," he replied just as softly, wrapping an arm around her shoulder to keep her close, as if it were the most natural gesture in the world. "Are you..." He hesitated a moment before continuing, not sure what to say, really. "Are you...okay?" he finally asked.

She nodded against his chest and inhaled a deep breath. "Oh, yes," she told him on a quiet sigh. "I'm very okay. I'm more okay than I have ever been in my entire life. I'm the absolute most okayest you'll ever see me. I guarantee."

Will chuckled at that. He was the absolute most okayest he'd ever been, too. He tangled his fingers in her silky hair and told himself there wasn't time for the two of them to make love again right now. They had too many things to talk about, too many things to explore, too many things to straighten out, too many things to make right.

But how, precisely, to go about that was a mystery to him at the moment.

"Tess," he began experimentally.

"Mmm-hmm?"

"I, um...I think we need to talk."

This time she was the one to chuckle. "I guess we didn't do much of that last night, did we?"

Heat wound through him at the memories of what they *did* do last night. "We were a little busy, yeah."

Her warm body felt so good pressing against his—their legs were entwined, and her arms were wrapped around his waist. He could scarcely tell where she ended and he began, so thorough had their union of the night before been. And he realized then that he liked the feeling of being utterly and irrevocably joined with her. He liked it a lot. It felt good. It felt...right.

"But we do need to talk," he said again.

"Mmm," she murmured sleepily. "Okay. Later. You

feel so good, I just want to lie here and hold you—and be held by you—for a while.''

''No, Tess, not later,'' he said, even though a part of him wanted nothing more than to do exactly as she suggested. The subtle movement of her body alongside his was making that conversation he had thought so important seem considerably less so. In spite of that he insisted, ''This morning. Now.''

She must have detected the note of concern in his voice, because she pushed herself away from him, far enough that she could gaze upon his face. By now there was enough light spilling into the room that Will could see her clearly, and the expression on her face was one of obvious confusion.

''What?'' she asked. ''What's wrong?''

He wanted to tell her that nothing was wrong, that, in fact, everything in his life suddenly felt more right than it ever had felt before. But he couldn't quite shake the notion that he had committed some egregious error by making love to her last night. As wonderful as the experience had been, it had come about under false pretenses.

Will had been thinking that Tess was pregnant. More specifically, he had been thinking she was pregnant by another man. He had assumed she still had feelings of some kind for that other man. As strange as it seemed, Will found things between him and Tess to be more complicated now that the other man was *out* of the picture—now that the other man had never even been in the picture—than things had been before.

Because suddenly Tess didn't have feelings for someone else. Presumably, she'd never had feelings for someone else. Which could only mean she had feelings for Will. Only Will. And maybe, just maybe, those feelings weren't generated by some capricious crush. Maybe they were generated by something infinitely more significant. Instead of relieving him, though, the realization of that only compounded his confusion.

Last night he had been the first man to make love to Tess. She had given him the most precious gift a woman could give to a man. The repercussions of that were still rippling through him and were messing with his thinking—big-time. He just wasn't sure he even *wanted* to know what it all meant.

"Last night," he began. But no more words followed those two that might help him out. Which wasn't exactly surprising, he had to admit. In spite of knowing that he and Tess needed to talk, Will still had no idea precisely what to say.

So Tess came to his aid. "Last night was wonderful," she told him, filling in the blanks and smiling the sweetest, most serene smile he had ever seen. When she looked at him like that, she was positively beatific, and Will felt blessed in a way he had never felt before.

"Yeah, it was," he agreed. Then, before he lost his nerve, he hurried on, "But, Tess, it shouldn't have happened. Not the way it did."

Her smile fell. "How can you say that? It was perfect. It was everything a first time should be."

"Which is exactly my point," he told her. "I didn't know it was your first time. If I had, I wouldn't have…you know…so hard that first time. I would have been more careful. Why didn't you tell me?"

"Because I knew you would be careful," she said without hesitation. "And I didn't want you careful. I wanted you the way you always are."

"You should have told me, Tess," he insisted.

She did hesitate a moment this time before replying. "Then you should have asked," she said softly.

"I didn't think I needed to."

"And that's exactly why I didn't tell you."

Had he thought he was confused before? Now he really didn't understand what was going on. "What are you talking about?"

Tess pushed herself away from him and sat up straight, arranging the sheet around her shoulders. In spite of her efforts, though, one side of it still fell down over her arm, nearly to her elbow. He tried not to notice the faint red marks on her tender flesh that must have been caused by the scratch of his beard, but that was exactly where he focused his gaze.

He had marked her last night, he realized. He hadn't meant to, but he had just the same. And, man, why was the knowledge of that so incredibly...so incredibly...*arousing?*

"Will," she began intently, "you readily believed that I was the kind of woman who would rush into a relationship with some guy and get pregnant as a result. Don't deny it." She hastened on when he opened his mouth to do just that. "You did. You wouldn't have believed me last night if I'd told you I was a virgin. It just would have complicated matters, and we would have ended up arguing, and I didn't want to argue with you." She paused a telling moment before continuing, "I wanted to make love with you. And I knew it wouldn't happen if I told you the truth."

"Oh, Tess." It was a lame response, but Will could think of nothing else to say.

What a mess he'd made of things. He never should have doubted her word in the first place. He never should have bought into the rumors. He should have realized from the start that Tess wasn't the kind of woman who would get into a situation like the one everybody had thought she was in. Will knew Tess. He knew she wasn't like that. So why had he believed what everyone else had said about her, instead of believing her?

Maybe, he thought, it was because something inside him wanted to think she *was* capable of that kind of behavior. Maybe it was because something inside him had wanted her to indulge in that kind of behavior with him. Maybe it was because he *wanted* Tess Monahan. Wanted her to be a sexual animal, and not the kid sister of his best friend.

And now she was. She was most definitely a sexual animal—in more ways than one. And she was certainly more to him now than his best friend's kid sister. She was his lover. She might very well be the mother of his child. Will was responsible for that. He had to be responsible for her, too.

"Tess, we didn't use any protection last night," he blurted out before he could stop himself. "I thought you were pregnant, and I knew you weren't promiscuous, and I'm not promiscuous, either, so I didn't see the need to use a condom. And I assume, since until last night you weren't sexually active, that you didn't use anything yourself."

She shook her head slowly. "No. I didn't even think about it. Last night all I could think about was you. About how much I wanted you. It just never occurred to me that... I'm sorry," she said softly.

"It's my responsibility," he said, voicing aloud his earlier thoughts. "Don't blame yourself."

"It was my responsibility, too, Will," she pointed out. Vehemently, he couldn't help but note. "There were two of us in this bed last night, you know."

"But I was the one who should have taken the initiative to use something. I'm the man."

She gaped at him, clearly outraged by his comment. "Hey, *I'm* the woman. *I'm* the one who's going to suffer the consequences more than you. *I* should have taken the initiative."

"Tess, you didn't know—"

"Just because I never made love before last night, that doesn't mean I'm ignorant. I'm a child of the seventies, Will. I know about sex and babies and HIV. Last night I was unforgivably careless. I should have taken precautions. The only reason I didn't was because—" She halted abruptly, as if unwilling to say what she had intended to say.

"Because...?" he prodded.

She sighed with much resignation. "Because I was with you."

"So if I had been someone else, you would have remembered?" he asked dubiously.

She met his gaze levelly, intently. "If you had been someone else, I never would have gotten into this bed in the first place."

That revelation, he decided, was something he should probably contemplate later, when he was alone. Right now they really did have other things to get settled.

"Tess, you could be pregnant," he said again.

"I don't think so," she told him. "The timing really wasn't right. I'm probably not."

"But that's no guarantee, is it?"

"No," she said. "It's not."

"There's a very real possibility, however remote, that you could've gotten pregnant last night."

With clear reluctance, she conceded, "I suppose so."

"Which means we need to do something about it."

She eyed him warily. "Define *do something*."

Might as well just spit it out, Darrow, he told himself. "Get married," he told her. "Tess, I think we should get married."

Nine

Tess widened her eyes in disbelief. "Get married?" she echoed incredulously. "*Get married?* Are you serious?"

Will nodded. "If you're pregnant, we need to do right by the baby and make sure it's legit. I don't want you to have to endure any more talk about single motherhood than you've already had to suffer. So I think we should get married. Right away, too, so there won't be any speculation about the timing. This way we could tell people you got pregnant on our honeymoon."

She expelled a soft sound of disbelief, then shook her head slowly, her gaze never leaving his. "That's it?" she said. "That's why you want to marry me? To make our baby—and there might not even be a baby—legitimate?"

"Hey, it's a hell of a good reason," he told her, sounding defensive.

"But is it the only reason?" she asked.

Will's expression went immediately shuttered at the

question. "Well…yeah," he said. "It'd be the honorable thing to do."

Honorable, Tess repeated to herself as she watched all her fragile hopes and dreams go up in smoke. For all of two minutes she had been able to envision turning her fantasy of a life with Will into a reality, but now she was going to have to let it go for good. Yes, he had just proposed marriage to her, and yes, that was what she had been dreaming about for years, the thing she wanted more than she had ever wanted anything in her entire life. But the only reason he was doing it was because he wanted to be honorable. *Honorable.*

How *dare* he?

Ever since the night he'd come to her house for dinner, when they'd spent the entire evening in quiet conversation, when he'd seemed so close to giving her a kiss good-night, she had been thinking that maybe, just maybe, Will was starting to fall for her in much the same way she had fallen for him. She had been thinking that maybe, just maybe, once he realized she wasn't pregnant with a mobster's child—and, hey, what better way to make him realize that than by letting him be the first, the only, to make love to her—that there might be a chance for the two of them to build something special, romantically speaking.

What she hadn't been thinking was that once they *had* built something special, romantically speaking—and what could possibly be more special than making love?— Will would snuff the romance right out of it by becoming, of all things, *honorable.*

Boy, you think you know a guy…

The last thing Tess wanted from Will was his honor. The first thing she wanted was his love. But all he was evidently able, or willing, to give her was the honor thing. Because love didn't seem to appear in his vocabulary—or anywhere else—at all.

"No," she said simply in response to his suggestion.

For a moment he seemed not to have heard her, because he only stared at her in dumbfounded silence. Then, very softly, he replied, "What?"

"I said no," she reiterated, with a bit more vigor this time. "I won't marry you."

His reaction was another one of those mystified silences, followed by an even softer, "But last night—"

"Last night," she interrupted him, "was about a lot more than maybe making a baby. At least it was to me."

"But—"

"And if the only reason you want us to be together is because there might be a child involved... Well, that's just wrong, is what that is."

It broke Tess's heart to tell him that, to turn down his offer, however misguided it had been. Nothing would have made her happier than walking down the aisle with Will and committing her life to his forever and ever and ever. But she wanted that to happen because he loved her and didn't want to live without her—the same way she loved him. She wanted him to want *her,* not just the child they might make together.

And the chances were good, anyway, that she wasn't pregnant. The timing really was all off, which may have been at the back of her mind last night, when it never occurred to her to use some form of protection. She had been with Will last night, so no protection had seemed necessary. Now, with the light of day creeping over the horizon and into her brain, she realized the folly of that decision. She was foolish not to have taken some precautions. But she truly hadn't thought any would be necessary.

Foolish girl, she thought again. Foolish, foolish, foolish. And not just for overlooking protection last night. But for a wealth of other reasons, too.

She was foolish to think that Will Darrow might ever come to love her. Even if he'd finally stopped viewing her as Finn Monahan's kid sister, even if he'd come to her bed and made sweet, tender love to her, even if he'd proposed marriage in an effort to be honorable...

He didn't love her. Not the way a man was supposed to love a woman when asking her to share her life with him. That much was obvious. And if he didn't love her after what the two of them had just shared, after the gift she had just bestowed upon him, after hearing her say the words herself, then he wasn't going to fall in love with her.

"I think you should go," she said softly. Somehow, she managed not to choke on the suggestion.

She tugged the sheet more securely around her shoulders, suddenly feeling the need to cover herself. Unfortunately, in doing so, she also pulled much of the sheet from Will, leaving his entire chest and one naked hip exposed. He truly was one glorious specimen of manhood, she couldn't help noting again. She could scarcely believe she had claimed that body with her own the night before.

And she could scarcely believe it wouldn't be happening again. But it wouldn't happen again. There was no reason to continue pursuing something that was clearly pointless.

For a minute she thought Will would argue with her, and a part of her almost hoped that he would. But he didn't. He only set his jaw firmly and tossed aside the sheet. Then, heedless of his nudity—and in total and complete silence—he picked up his scattered clothes and headed for the bathroom across the hall.

Tess sat silently, too, in the middle of her bed, tangled in her quickly cooling sheets, listening to the sounds of Will leaving—briefly running water, the squeak of the bathroom door, the hasty thump-thump-thump of footsteps on the stairs, the slam of the front door behind him. She tried neither to stop him nor to hasten his departure, possibly because she had no idea how she should act. In scarcely twelve hours' time, she'd gone from soaring through her wildest dreams to seeing those dreams shattered and trampled. From utter joy to total desolation. From seeing a future filled with love and devotion to realizing hers held only loneliness and isolation instead.

Never in her life had she felt so empty and alone. She didn't even have her nonexistent baby or her fictional lover to keep her company anymore. Will knew the truth. It wouldn't be long before all of Marigold knew. If not because Will told them, then because she herself showed no signs of being pregnant. And once the truth of her situation was finally out there, Tess would be right back where she'd started from.

Except that nothing would ever be the same again.

She'd just given away something she could never get back, and she'd given it to a man who didn't even know what it meant. Not just her virginity, but her heart and her love. Will had taken them all last night. And Tess knew they would be with him forever. She was his completely, eternally.

Whether he wanted her or not.

Will managed to make it through one full week without returning to Tess's house before he started thinking that maybe it wouldn't hurt to go check on her and make sure she was okay. Seven full days. Seven very full, very long days. Seven very full, very long, very boring days. Seven very full, very long, very boring, very cranky days.

He didn't exactly *enjoy* those seven days, nor was any of them particularly productive. And, okay, maybe he had been thinking about going to check on Tess *before* the end of those seven days, like maybe, oh...five minutes after leaving her house that morning after they'd made love. But he didn't think about it *seriously* until he'd made it through seven full days. And he did make it through seven full days. Eventually.

Just because every one of those days seemed to be interminable, well... That was just because his frame of reference, timewise, had been completely messed up. Probably because that one night he'd spent with Tess had immediately started to seem as though it had happened a lifetime ago. Probably because that single night had felt as though it lasted a lifetime itself. A really nice lifetime, too, if truth be told. One that had been full and bright and happy. In one night Will had lived a good life with Tess. But now that life was over. Because she had told him to leave.

Oh, you are such *a sap, Darrow,* he said to himself one morning as he sipped his coffee and waited for his first customer to arrive. Both Benjy and Kim were due to come in for work later, but right now, at 6:30 a.m., it was just Will, and he was glad for that. As usual, he wasn't in the mood to be amiable or agreeable. In fact, he hadn't been in the mood to be either of those things since he'd left Tess's house eight mornings ago—not that he was counting or anything. And really, he doubted he would ever feel either of those things again. Certainly not as long as things between him and Tess were left so up in the air.

Which must have been why he started thinking that morning—seriously this time—about going to see her and make sure she was okay. They'd managed pretty well to avoid each other this week, Will by staying close to home and Tess by staying wherever she had stayed to avoid him. But Marigold was a small town, where everybody knew everybody. He and Tess couldn't hide out forever, certainly not during the summer, when people just naturally got out and about. Eventually they were bound to run into each other again. And when they did, it was going to be awkward.

Especially if Tess was pregnant.

Because in spite of her assurances to the contrary, Will just couldn't shake the idea of such a possibility becoming a reality. What if her calculations had been off? What if she really was pregnant? What if, just when the incorrect talk of her being pregnant was finally coming to an end, she started showing and people knew for a fact that she *was* expecting? Then they'd *really* start wondering about the father. And Will wasn't about to let Tess face something like that alone. He would come forward with the truth, of course.

But what if that didn't change anything? he thought further. What if Tess still refused to marry him? What if she wanted to raise their child by herself? Will couldn't let her do that, either. Not only would he feel responsible for the baby, he'd want to take an active role as father. It would be his child, too. He was entitled. Hey, who did Tess think she was, trying to keep him from his own flesh and blood?

Will squeezed his eyes shut tight and told himself to stop being so irrational. Tess wasn't trying to keep him from his own flesh and blood. There was no way to know right now how she would react to a baby, or to his desire to be involved in raising a child. She might not even be pregnant. *Probably* wasn't pregnant, he quickly corrected himself.

But what if she was?

He sighed heavily and swallowed the last of his coffee and tried to remember how he'd made such a mess of things. It had happened, he realized, because he hadn't been able to resist Tess that night. Something he hadn't been able to control had just compelled him to make love to her. She had just felt so good, had made everything seem so right.

Funny, now, how everything suddenly felt so wrong instead.

Tess was folding laundry in the living room when she heard the familiar rumble of Will Darrow's pickup truck and halted midfold. She'd been wondering which of them would be the first to come out of hiding, and she wasn't really surprised that it was Will. Although she was beginning to run low on diet Pepsi and Oreos—so it wouldn't have been long before she would have been forced to brave the supermarket and risk running into him.

Now, however, it looked like she wouldn't have to worry about that. No, now all she had to worry about was seeing him in the privacy of her own home, where they'd be all alone, free from prying eyes, close to her bedroom, where just about anything might happen.

She suddenly wished she had ventured out long before now.

Because if there was one thing she had learned in the past week, it was that not seeing Will was a pretty hideous activity. And if there was another thing she'd learned, it was that living without him was going to be even worse. Oh, and there was also a third thing she'd learned—that she missed him. A lot. Okay, and there was one more thing she had learned, too, making it that she had actually learned four things in the past week. And that fourth thing was that she couldn't possibly be held responsible for her actions once she did see Will again, due to that missing-him-a-lot thing under lesson number three.

Nevertheless she finished folding the pajama bottoms draped over her arm and laid them atop the rest of the color load, then smoothed a hand over her sleeveless pink jumper. She hadn't worn yellow for a week now. It reminded her too much of Will.

She had just tugged free the rubber band from her ponytail and was still fluffing out her hair—only because the rubber band had been pulling uncomfortably, that was all—when the screen door rattled under three rapid knocks. She inhaled a deep, steadying breath and strode forward, then paused at the door without opening it.

"Hi," she said softly through the screen.

Will studied her intently for a moment, then echoed, just as softly, "Hi."

An awkward silence followed for a few moments, wherein all each of them did was study the other's face. Will looked tired, agitated, impatient, much the same way Tess had felt all week. His navy T-shirt, emblazoned with the words Theo's Gym in fading gold letters, hung untucked over equally faded jeans. His dark hair looked as if it had recently been combed—then immediately ruined by restless fingers. All in all, he didn't appear to care much for his appearance. And that just made him all the more attractive for some reason.

"Can I come in?" he finally asked.

Instinctively Tess lifted a hand to unlatch the screen,

but she hesitated before completing the action. "I don't know that it's such a good idea," she told him, dropping her hand back to her side.

He arched his dark eyebrows in surprise. Clearly this was not the response he had expected from her. "Why not?" he demanded roughly.

Because you want to be honorable, she thought. *Because you don't love me the way I love you.*

"I just think we've said everything we need to say, that's all," she replied.

He fixed his gaze on hers. "That's funny. 'Cause I don't feel like we've said nearly enough. Let me in, Tess."

And why did he make it sound as though he was commanding to be let in to a lot more than her house? she wondered.

She shook her head slowly. "I was just...on my way out," she lied.

His gaze never left hers. "Let me in, Tess," he repeated more intently.

"I'm on my way...out," she said again, with even less conviction this time.

He dropped his gaze pointedly down to her feet—her *bare* feet—which he could see through the full-view screen door. "Aren't you forgetting something?" he asked, returning his attention to her face.

She nibbled her lip nervously, and his attention immediately shifted to the small gesture. His pupils expanded, and his own lips parted softly, as if he were remembering, very well, the way their mouths had fitted together that night they'd—

Oh, dear.

"I mean, um..." she tried again. "I, uh...I *will* be on

my way out. In just a, uh, a few minutes. As soon as I put on my shoes.''

He knew she was lying. She could tell. In spite of that he lifted his gaze to hers again and told her, ''Fine. I'll drive you wherever you need to go.''

Tess sighed, feeling her reserve slipping away. She knew she was a lousy liar, but still told him, ''That won't be necessary. I'm not going far.''

Well that, at least, was the truth. She really wasn't going far. In fact, she was going nowhere. With this conversation, with her life or with her feelings for Will.

''Let me in, Tess,'' he said a third time.

And that, of course, was the charm. There was no way she could deny him, no way she *would* deny him. Not just because of the plaintive pleading in his voice, but because she really didn't want him to go. Seeing him again, even with circumstances being what they were, even if it was only for a little while, was just too good an opportunity to pass up.

Slowly she lifted the latch, but it was Will, not she, who opened the door. The moment the hook was free of its loop, he grabbed the handle and tugged forward, as if he feared she might change her mind. Then he stepped inside so swiftly Tess scarcely had time to step out of the way. In fact, she didn't step out of the way. She stumbled out of the way. Or, at least, she would have stumbled. If Will hadn't snaked out an arm to catch her.

And looped it around her waist.

And pulled her close.

''Hi,'' he said again, his voice a quiet murmur.

''Hi,'' she replied, in much the same tone.

She curled her fingers into loose fists and settled them gingerly against his chest. Inevitably, though, they unfolded, spreading open until her palms lay flat against the warm expanse. Beneath her fingertips, Tess could feel the rapid, irregular pulsing of his heart, and she knew that he was as uncertain and anxious about this meeting as she was. Somehow that made her feel a little better. Not a lot. But a little.

Hey, it was a start.

Will cupped both of his hands on her waist, then let them slide slowly to the flare of her hips before stopping. But he didn't pull her closer, and Tess wondered if that might be because he was worried about his reception in that department.

He did, however, say, "I've missed you."

And that went a long way toward potentially repairing some of the little tears in her heart.

"I've missed you, too," she told him.

"I still think we need to talk."

"I still think we've covered what we needed to cover. If you're only here to be honorable, Will—"

"That's not why I'm here."

"Then why?"

He smiled. "I never finished painting the ba—" He broke off, and his smile fell some. But he rallied it quickly and amended, "I never finished the painting job I began. And you know how I am about unfinished business. I hate leaving a job undone."

She nodded. That much was true. But it wouldn't be a problem here. "Sean finished it himself last week. He hates leaving a job undone, too."

Will's smile fell completely at that. "Oh. Well. He should have called me. I would have helped him."

Her gaze skittered to the side, focusing on something over Will's left shoulder. "He was going to. But I, um…I told him not to bother you. That you wouldn't be available."

Will said nothing for a moment, then, slowly, "But that's not true," he told her. "I would have been available. For painting," he hastily added, as if it were important that she understand the distinction.

She nodded. "Well, anyway, it doesn't matter, because the job is done now."

"Then I guess there's no reason for me to be here, is there?" he asked.

His posture belied his words, however, because the fingers curved over her hips curled tighter, and he pulled Tess forward. She went willingly, without thought, without care, moving her hands up to his shoulders, his broad, solid, strong shoulders. One more small step, she thought, and she could nestle her head into the hollow of his throat, press her mouth to the warm skin peeking out of his shirt collar. Unconsciously she skimmed a hand upward, cupping her fingers over his nape, loving the feel of his warm flesh beneath her palm, and the sensation of silky hair skimming over the back of her hand.

"Tess," he said softly, drawing one hand upward to strum it over her rib cage, "I really do think we need to talk."

She was beginning to think he was right on that score, beginning to think that maybe she'd been mistaken about his feelings for her. Because he seemed so tender right now, so caring, so...loving. Maybe there *was* a chance for the two of them, she told herself as a spark of hope ignited in her belly. Maybe he *did* have feelings for her that mirrored hers for him. Maybe he *could* come to—

"I'm worried you might be pregnant," he said.

And in doing so, tossed a bucket of ice water on that tiny, hopeful flame that had begun to burn more brightly, drenching it thoroughly.

Tess chose her words carefully. "You are, huh?"

He took a step closer, bringing his body flush with hers, and moved one hand to the small of her back, splaying his fingers wide. Then he lifted his chin to tuck her head beneath it, pulling her closer still. Tess let him do it for two reasons. Number one, because she didn't want him to see the faint tears forming in her eyes with the exquisite torture of being so close to him again, knowing he didn't really want her. And, number two, because she didn't want to see the pity etched on his face when he told her how honorable he needed to be.

And for a third reason, too, she had to admit as she spread her own hands open over the warm, solid expanse of his back. Because she was just selfish enough to want to experience his embrace one final time. Even if it were happening for all the wrong reasons, and however fleeting it might be.

"I know you said the timing wasn't right for you to get pregnant," he began, "and that it wasn't likely to happen. But, Tess, for the past week, I just haven't been able to stop thinking about how you might have a baby growing inside you. About how I might become a father. About what all that might entail."

How ironic, Tess thought. Because what she hadn't been able to stop thinking about all week was how Will had felt stretched out alongside her, atop her, behind her, inside her. About how his mouth had felt so fiercely fastened to hers, about how their fingers had felt so erotically entwined, about what a perfect fit their bodies had been, and what a perfect match their hearts had seemed to be. About how she hadn't thought it would be possible to love him more than she did, but that making love with him had only magnified her already profound emotions.

What she *hadn't* thought about, even once, was a baby. Memories of Will had superseded any and all ideas on that count. Clearly, however, Tess wasn't such a primary concern for him. The baby was. That was why he had come back today. Not for Tess, but for the child they might have created together.

She was about to push him away when she felt his hands move lightly over her back, idly caressing, tenderly stroking, as if he truly enjoyed having her right where she was. Then again, he'd never said he didn't want to touch her, she reminded herself. He'd never said he didn't want to make love to her again, or even that he wanted to stop seeing her. Clearly, he still cared about her. Judging by the way he was holding her now, Tess couldn't dispute that.

But his reasons for touching her so intimately didn't mirror her reasons for wanting him to continue. He cared about her for the same reason he had always cared about her—because she was Finn's little sister. And, too, because she might potentially be the mother of his child. It wasn't because he loved her. Not the way a man was supposed to love a woman. Not the way she loved him.

"Will," she said, amazed that her voice reflected none of the emptiness or melancholy that she was feeling.

Instead of letting her finish what she was going to say, though, he pushed on. "When, um...when will you know for sure?" he asked. "About the baby, I mean. How long before you know whether or not you're—"

"I'm not," she said shortly.

The hands he had been skimming lightly over her back and neck and shoulders suddenly went utterly still. "You're not?"

"No. I'm not."

"Are you sure?"

"I'm sure."

"Oh."

She swallowed hard, but couldn't quite bring herself to pull away. Surprisingly, Will didn't try to pull away, either. Instead he continued to hold her, if not quite as close as before. Gradually, though, his hands slid down to link loosely at the small of her back again. And little by little Tess realized he was beginning to withdraw.

"I found out yesterday," she told him. "In fact, my period came a little earlier than usual. I'm not pregnant, Will. You're not going to be a father. You can stop worrying now."

For a single, heart-stopping moment, he didn't move, didn't say a word, didn't seem to breathe. And in that single, heart-stopping moment Tess wondered if maybe she'd been wrong. Maybe he really had come for some other reason than that he was worried she was pregnant. Maybe he really had come because he missed her. Maybe there was some hope, however small, that they could—

He took a step away from her then, and whatever tiny, infinitesimal hope she might have clung to was washed away completely. Will had come because he thought she was pregnant—there was no way she could deny that now. It wasn't because he had wanted to see her again. It wasn't because he couldn't live without her. It was because he had been afraid she was carrying his child, a child for whom he would feel obligated to provide.

Will had come because he had thought Tess was an obligation. Not because he loved her.

"Well, I guess that's good news, isn't it?" he said. But the words were stiff and cool in preparation for what she was sure would be his hasty departure.

"Yeah, it is," she agreed. Though for some reason she felt oddly disappointed when she thought more about it. Empty, almost. Sad. It made no sense. Becoming pregnant by Will would have been the worst thing that could happen to her. She really would have had to face the stigma and hardship of single motherhood, had that become a reality.

Worse, she would have had to continue to live in the same town with the baby's father, knowing he didn't want her the way she wanted him. And Will would be the kind of man who wanted to play an active role in the life of his child. There was no way she could have avoided him. And even if he had continued to want her—sexually, if not emotionally—there was no way she could have married him, knowing he didn't love her.

So, yes, it was definitely a good thing she wasn't pregnant. It was just too bad she couldn't quite convince herself of that.

In spite of her certainty where his motivation was concerned, she couldn't help asking, "Is that why you came here today? Because you were still worried I might be pregnant?"

That seemed to stump him, because the look he gave her then was rife with confusion. "Well, yeah," he finally said. He shrugged, but there was nothing much careless in the gesture. Instead, he seemed to be trying to dislodge—without much success—a heavy weight from his back. "Why else?"

Why else indeed? she asked herself, her heart sinking even lower than it had been before. Certainly, there was still something there between them, something warm and vivid and perhaps even substantial. But it wasn't love, she thought. Not on his part at any rate. And now that he knew she wasn't pregnant, there wouldn't even be obligation.

Not that she wanted to be his obligation, she thought further. But she sure would have liked to be his love.

"So you can go home and rest easy," she told him.

She battled the urge to straighten and cross her arms over her midsection, suddenly feeling inexplicably cold. "You're off the hook," she said further, injecting a lightness into her tone that she was nowhere close to feeling. "You can celebrate the fact that you're not going to become a father. Whoopee."

Before Will could withdraw any more than he already had, Tess disentangled herself from what was left of his embrace—it wasn't particularly hard to do, after all, seeing as how he offered absolutely no objection—then took a small step backward. Then she took another. And another. And another.

There, she thought as she put the distance of the entire foyer between them, *see how easy it is? You just have to take one step at a time, that's all.*

When she braved a glance at Will, she was stunned to see how stricken he looked. Funny, but if she hadn't known better, she would have almost thought he was upset about her not being pregnant. Which made about as much sense as *Tess* being upset about not being pregnant. Which, of course, wasn't the case at all. Therefore, Will couldn't possibly be upset about that, either.

Could he?

Of course not.

It was just the whole awkwardness of the situation that made him look the way he did, she told herself. Things between the two of them were bound to be uncomfortable now, and that was going to create some turbulence whenever the Monahans got together—which was often. Will was practically family, and their family was close. This new uneasiness between them was going to be like a wedge planted firmly into the Monahan infrastructure. It just wasn't going to be the same at all.

And it was bound to change Will's relationship with

Finn, too. Not that Tess would ever breathe a word of what had happened between her and Will to her oldest brother—or to anyone else for that matter. But Will would be carrying around the knowledge for the rest of his life, and he was the kind of man who would feel unaccountably guilty for doing what he had done.

He was, after all, *honorable*. Taking the virginity of his best friend's kid sister was bound to make him feel like a heel, to say the least. The fact that it was only a one-night stand would just exacerbate the problem. And feeling it necessary to keep the whole thing secret from his best friend would doubtless make it even worse. There was sure to be some tension in his friendship with Finn for a while. At least until Will could forget about what he and Tess had done.

He expelled a restless, almost angry, sigh. Then he fisted one hand tightly and shoved the other ruthlessly through his hair. "Tess, I don't... I wasn't... I didn't... I'm not..." Obviously unable to choose a thought and go with it, Will clamped his mouth shut tight again and dropped both hands to his sides.

He looked so uncomfortable that Tess wanted to give his hand an affectionate pat and tell him that it was okay, that she would get over it, that everything would be all right. But she'd be lying if she said any of those things. So she only forced a fractured smile and strode on shaky legs to the front door. Without a word she pushed it open and stood back in silent invitation for Will to leave.

For a moment he hesitated, as if he were going to perpetuate his "We need to talk" stance. Then, clearly feeling as hopeless as she, he took a few steps forward. He paused right at the threshold, however, and turned to gaze at her one last time. Before she realized what he was doing, he lifted a hand to skim the backs of his knuckles gingerly over her cheek, once, twice, three times.

The keen heat and flash of desire that shot through Tess at his gesture nearly overwhelmed her, and instinctively she lifted her own hand to cover his. Before she could touch him, however, he withdrew his hand and dropped it back to his side. Then he moved forward again, onto the porch and down the steps, without a backward glance.

Even after he had climbed into his truck and started the engine, he never spared her another glance. Tess closed the door and, through the screen, she watched him leave, her gaze never leaving his truck until it had rounded the corner at the end of the street—with far more speed than was prudent.

Would that she could escape so easily, she thought. But no matter how fast or how far she drove in her lifetime, she knew she would never be able to completely leave Will.

Without even realizing she was doing it, she opened her hand over her empty womb and sighed.

Ten

In the two weeks that followed his final expulsion from Tess's house, Will became exceedingly cranky. It was a condition duly noted by everyone in Marigold, because Will Darrow was never, ever cranky. He was the most easy-going, affable guy a person could ever hope to meet, a man whose feathers just never got ruffled. So seeing him cranky roused more than a little concern among the local citizenry. Even Abigail Torrance stopped bringing him casseroles, because he told her at one point that her tuna noodle surprise had lost its magic. Needless to say, Abigail had been stunned.

It was the same reaction everyone in Marigold experienced whenever they ran across Will. Even Finn Monahan got fed up one day and asked his friend flat-out what the hell had gotten into him. Will winced in response, bit his tongue against saying it wasn't so much what had gotten into *him* as it was what—or rather, *who*—he had gotten into himself. Saying that would have been crass and rude and gotten him punched in the mouth, should Finn figure out who the *who* was that Will had gotten into. Worse, it would have roused memories he would just as soon not have roused.

So when Finn asked his question that hot Fourth of July, Will just snarled at his friend and told him to go away.

"I'm not going anywhere until you tell me what's wrong," Finn insisted. "You haven't been yourself for two weeks now. And Sean told me you never showed up at Tessie's to finish painting the baby's room. He had to do it all by himself. It's not like you to shirk, Will."

"Yeah, well, I was going to help him finish painting," Will retorted with much crankiness. "But Tess sorta pulled in the welcome mat on me there. She told Sean I was unavailable before she even asked me if I was—I wasn't, by the way," he interjected, crankily, at that, "*and* she didn't tell me Sean was coming until after the job was done."

Although he didn't see any reason to mention them to Finn, Will still had flashbacks over the day he had gone to Tess's house to see her. He kept recalling how she'd looked so beautiful and sad and lonely and beautiful when she'd answered the door, and how, ultimately, nothing had changed between them. Yes, something in her expression that day had made him want to come inside and make love to her again, until the shadows darkening her eyes disappeared. Something in her eyes had made him want to take back everything he'd said about being honorable and just lose himself in her warmth and sweetness for days on end.

But Will hadn't done that. Because he hadn't gone to her house to make love to her. No, the only reason he had gone over there was to check on her, to make sure she was okay. But, of course, she *hadn't* been okay. Because, thanks to the night the two of them had spent at Tess's house, *everything* was different now. And no matter how hard they might try, they couldn't change anything back.

They couldn't go back in time and alter the fact that the two of them had made love and totally messed up the friendship they'd had for so many years. Will couldn't give Tess back her virginity, nor could he quite convince himself that she had surrendered it to a man for whom she felt nothing more than infatuation, infatuation that would eventually fade.

Okay, so he'd been the first man to make love to her. Fine. But had he been her first because she genuinely loved him? Or because she had simply made it a habit all her life of wanting him to be first? Love or infatuation? Will just didn't know.

What was most important, he tried to assure himself, was that Tess wasn't pregnant. That meant she wouldn't have to face the stigma of single motherhood. It meant that, soon enough, everyone in Marigold would realize how wrong they'd all been about her. And it meant that Will didn't have to lie awake in bed at night anymore, worrying about doing the honorable thing. No, now he could lie awake in bed at night, worrying about a host of other things instead.

Honorable, hell, he thought now. The last thing he considered himself to be these days was honorable. Two weeks of replaying his and Tess's lovemaking over and over and *over* again in his brain sorta kept a man from feeling honorable. Instead it made a man feel damned depressed—among other things—because the woman he wanted to be with had asked him to leave. Twice.

He told himself he should be relieved to find out that she wasn't pregnant, but something about the news had bothered Will a lot. He still had no idea why. Nor could he understand why he continued to think about marrying Tess, even though there was no reason to do so now. Nobody but he and she knew they had spent the night together. There was no baby to make legitimate. So why did he keep thinking about the two of them having a future together? Hell, it wasn't like the two of them were in love. Tess was nurturing a crush, and Will cared for her the way he had always cared for her. But that wasn't the kind of love that made a marriage.

Was it?

Of course not.

"Tess actually threw you out that day?" Finn asked, bringing Will's thoughts back to the present.

"Yeah, she did," he replied in a clipped tone.

Instead of being outraged, which was how Will had felt at the time—and how he continued to feel two weeks later—Finn only chuckled merrily. "Oh, man. I can't believe Tessie would actually shut you out."

"Yeah, well, she did, okay?"

"God, what did you do to her?" Finn asked, still laughing. "Musta been pretty awful to have her slamming the door on the love of her life."

"She didn't exactly slam the—" Will halted when Finn's words finally registered in his brain. What the hell was he talking about? "What the hell are you talking about?" he echoed his thoughts aloud. "What do you mean 'the love of her life'? I'm not the love of Tess's life."

"Well, not anymore, obviously," Finn said, his laughter fading to a broad smile. Then his smile, too, broke off, and he gazed at Will in stunned disbelief. "You mean you didn't know?"

Will shook his head, totally mystified. "Know what?"

Finn gaped at his friend. "My God, you *didn't* know."

"Know *what?*" Will demanded.

But all Finn said in response was, "Hell, Will, everybody in Marigold knows. How could you not know?"

"Know *what?*"

Finn expelled a soft sound of disbelief. "That Tess is in love with you."

"What?"

"She's always been in love with you, you jerk. What are you, blind?"

Will shook his head more vehemently. "Tess isn't in love with me," he countered. "She's had a crush on me, that's all. A crush."

"It may have been a crush when she was twelve," Finn acknowledged. "But it hasn't been a crush since she came home from college. I can't believe you didn't figure that out a long time ago."

"But—"

"I just never brought it up myself," Finn continued, oblivious to Will's—granted, minuscule—objection, "because I figured it was common knowledge and you were just trying to let her down gently by pretending you didn't know. I thought it was kind of nice of you, actually, to spare her feelings that way. I mean, yeah, there were times when I wished you'd return her feelings—it'd be great to have you as a brother-in-law. But I know—probably better than anybody in town—that you can't force someone to fall in love with someone else, just because it would make me—or rather, *you*—happy." Finn eyed Will with much curiosity. "But you really didn't know, did you? You really didn't know that Tess is in love with you.''

Will stared blindly at his friend as he tried to make sense of everything Finn was saying, as he tried to figure out what he was feeling inside. It wasn't just a crush? Tess was in love with him? Was that possible? Sure, the night they'd spent together had gone beyond incredible, but he'd just figured that had been because of…because of… Well…because of…

Because of what? he asked himself now. Because of the fact that Tess was in love with him? Because of the fact that *he* was in love with *her?* Was *that* possible?

"Are you sure about this?" he asked Finn.

Finn's smile returned, full-blown. "Oh, that whole pregnant-by-the-Mob thing may have thrown me temporarily, but…of course I'm sure." Then, very meaningfully, he added, "Why? Are you having second thoughts now about your reasons for making love to her?"

Hell, Will had never even had *first* thoughts about—

"Making love to her?" he echoed shallowly as something heavy and icy settled in his stomach. "You, uh…you know about that?"

Finn rolled his eyes. "Will. Please. Of course I know about that."

"And you're not going to…"

The corners of Finn's lips notched even higher. "Not going to what?" he asked innocently.

Will shrugged with totally fake nonchalance. "Oh, I don't know…not going to beat the hell outta me?"

Finn screwed up his face distastefully. "Will, please. Why would I do something like that to my best friend?"

"Gee, color me confused, but weren't you Monahan boys going to beat the hell outta the guy in the Witness Protection Program who knocked her up?"

"Oh, that."

"Yes, that."

"Well, of course we would have beaten the hell outta that guy. He didn't love Tess. You, on the other hand..."

"Me?"

"Will, please," Finn said again. "You're embarrassing yourself."

"Oh." Then, cautiously, he asked, "How did you, um...how did you know how I felt about Tess?"

Finn shrugged. "I could tell by the way you ruffle her hair."

Will arched his eyebrows in surprise, but said nothing.

"So what are you going to do now, Einstein?" Finn asked, his words tinged with laughter.

"I don't know," Will mumbled. His head was too full of speculation for him to know what he was even *thinking* about, let alone what he was going to *do*. So all he did was mutter another, totally honest, "I don't know."

Normally Tess very much looked forward to Marigold's annual Fourth of July celebration. Normally she packed a cooler for the day and met up with friends in Gardencourt Park, then spread her blanket near theirs by the gazebo to watch the people go by. Normally throughout the day she would enjoy the booths, the activities, the craft bazaar and the homemade refreshments. Normally by the time night fell she'd feel mellow and relaxed and ready for the extensive fireworks display.

Of course Tess hadn't felt normal for some time now. Not since she and Will had—

But she wasn't going to think about that anymore, was she? she interrupted herself before she could get started. No, she had promised herself two weeks ago, quite explicitly, that she simply would not waste any more time or brain power contemplating things that were way beyond the realm of possibility. Consequently she had abandoned her hope of colonizing space, had accepted the fact that there would never be a sugar-free chocolate that tasted good and had given up on ever marrying Will Darrow.

And she tried to continue on with her life in as routine—if somewhat abnormal—a fashion as possible.

This particular Fourth of July, however—not surprisingly—wasn't yielding Tess any of her usual, normal, fun. Although she had packed a cooler, she'd felt way too restless to spread a blanket anywhere and had spent the bulk of the day, so far, flitting from group to group and event to exhibit without lighting anywhere for very long. She hadn't even chatted much with her brothers, and she'd run into each of them at some point during the day.

Sean, especially, had been preoccupied, had obviously been busy staking a claim—or, at the very least, *trying* to stake a claim—on Autumn Pulaski. Which was strange, now that Tess thought about it, because it was common knowledge in Marigold that Autumn Pulaski, resident free spirit—*free spirit* being Marigold's way of saying *oddball*—never dated any man for more than a month—a lunar month, at that—no matter what. Sean might not be the type for long-term relationships—mostly because he wasn't the type for *any*-term relationships—but even he liked to stay with a woman long enough to... Well, long enough.

And Finn...

Oh, Finn. Her oldest brother had seemed to be enjoying a very funny joke at Tess's expense the whole time she was talking to him. Granted, he'd been holding a glass of Andy Duncan's home brew at the time, but even that didn't account for his strange behavior. Finn could drink any man in Marigold under the table, and had on more than one occasion.

But when Tess ran into him around midafternoon, he kept smiling this big, goofy smile and yakking on and on about how the sky was just *so blue* today, and the sun was just *so bright* today, and the birds were singing just *so sweetly* in the trees today, and wasn't it just such a *beautiful* day today, such a *lovely* day today, such a *gorgeous* day today, just the *perfect* kind of day, especially for lovers, and…

Tess had beaten a hasty retreat the moment Finn had stopped to take a breath. And she'd made a mental note not to drink any of Andy Duncan's home brew.

Hours later, as twilight began to fall, all the people who had been milling about in crowds all day began to fracture off into couples and families. Tess figured that was because they all wanted to be together as they enjoyed supper and shared their experiences of the day and watched the fireworks afterward.

Her first response to the observation was to feel a bit cheated, because she didn't have a family to fracture off with herself. Then she reminded herself that the Monahans were one of the closest-knit families in Marigold, probably in the state of Indiana, possibly in the entire United States of America. She had a great family. One of the best. For some reason, though, as she watched all those other families joining together, many of them with children in tow, she still felt strangely bereft.

A lot of those married couples and moms and dads were people she had gone to school with, Tess reflected. Some of her friends had been happily married for years, and several of them had young children. Although she was only twenty-six herself, she had stopped feeling like a restless youth some time ago. In her heart of hearts she was ready to settle down and start a family. She knew her whole life lay spread before her and that she could do with it whatever she wanted. But she wasn't an adventurer or a vagabond—she had no desire to do or live any other way than she was doing and living right now. Unless it was to do or live the way she was doing and living now...with someone at her side.

No, not someone, she corrected herself. Will Darrow. She wanted him by her side.

"Tess."

Hearing the rough, quiet utterance of her name, she spun around to find that, as if conjured by her deepest desires, Will was steadily approaching her. He had dressed up for the picnic, she thought with a smile. His blue jeans were only marginally faded, without a rip to be had; his white, short-sleeved oxford shirt was starched and pressed. His hair, for once, appeared not to have been ruthlessly handled, and he had clearly just recently shaved. He looked clean-cut and dapper, the epitome of small-town boy turned small-town man. And Tess's heart raced rampant at the sight of him.

"Hi," she said, her own voice sounding as rough and quiet as his did.

He took a final, cautious step forward, then halted. "Long time, no see," he told her.

"Only two weeks," she reminded him.

He covered the rest of the small distance in a few, deceptively careless, strides. When he stood before her, he thrust his hands into his front pockets, a gesture that seemed to be indicating he was open for...a number of things. "Like I said, long time."

Yes, Tess thought, it had been a long time. A very long time indeed. She'd never realized just how endless two weeks could be until now. Because in seeing Will again, she realized how empty and pointless those two weeks had been. She hadn't lived a moment during those weeks. She'd simply existed in some kind of vague time continuum that had no beginning, no ending, no meaning.

"You look pretty," he told her, nodding once toward her pale-peach sundress.

She, too, dropped her gaze to the garment, not so much to remind herself what it looked like, but because she didn't know what to make of the fire that was dancing in Will's eyes. Well, she knew what to make of it—she'd seen it before, after all. She just didn't know how to react to it now.

"Thanks," she finally said. She steered her own gaze from his feet back to his face, then smiled a bit nervously. "You, uh…you don't look so bad yourself."

He shrugged the compliment off. He clearly had something on his mind other than forming a mutual admiration society, as was made clear when he stated flat-out, "I've been looking for you since this afternoon, but I couldn't find you. Finn told me you were here, but I sure didn't see you anywhere. I was beginning to think I might never find you again."

Something in his voice—something that was at once fearful and hopeful—set Tess's pulse on the puree setting, sending her blood whirring through her veins at a dizzying pace. "I, um…I've been wandering around a lot," she told him.

He nodded, as if he understood. "Feeling restless?" he asked.

"Yeah. Kind of."

"Me, too."

Tess swallowed hard, wondering what she was supposed to say or do now. Something told her that Will had scripted this scene with a specific conclusion, and she couldn't tell yet whether or not she was performing her role correctly. She opened her mouth to ask for some kind of prompt or cue, when he lifted a hand to her face. He hesitated a moment before touching her, as if he wanted to give her a chance to stop him. But the last thing Tess wanted him to do was stop. So she only stood stock-still and waited.

She was rewarded by the gentle brush of his fingertips across her cheekbone, the merest, sweetest sensation she'd ever felt. Involuntarily she parted her lips and sucked in a surprised breath, but otherwise offered no response. Will didn't seem to know what to make of her reaction, but he didn't pull his hand back. In fact, he skimmed the pad of his thumb along her lower lip, once, twice, three times, until Tess didn't think she'd be able to survive the wave of heat that shot through her as a result.

His gaze was focused on her mouth as he told her, "You know, I don't think I've ever mentioned this to anyone before, but you can see the fireworks really, really well from the roof of the garage."

She smiled a tremulous little smile. Somewhere she found the strength to ask him, "No kidding?"

"No kidding."

"Gee, I would have thought you'd need to be sitting someplace up high or something."

"It's higher than the park," he reminded her. "And the view from here is always great."

"Well, that's true…"

"Imagine how much nicer it would be from the roof of the garage. Just the two of us. All alone."

Tess imagined. Boy, did she imagine. And she realized

Will was right. It could be very nice indeed. Just the two of them. All alone.

"I could spread a blanket for us," he offered.

"Yeah?" she murmured.

He nodded. "Maybe light a candle or two."

"It wouldn't spoil the view?" she asked softly.

"Nah. It'd actually make it better."

"Oh."

"And I keep a cooler of beer up there, too," he added, "just for nice nights like this one. I go up there to think sometimes. Clears my head."

"Up on the roof a lot, are you?"

He met her gaze unflinchingly. "Lately I have been, yeah."

Oh, my. "Had a lot to think about?" she asked him.

"Yup."

"Drawn any conclusions?"

He tilted his head to the side a bit and continued to stroke her lip. "Still working on them."

Tess's heart hammered harder, her blood raced faster, her knees began to go weak. "Need any help?" she said softly.

He shrugged. "I guess I could use a research assistant."

"I have a degree in education, you know. Two of them," she hastily clarified.

He grinned. "Do tell."

"I'm really good at research."

"It's a very specific kind of research," he cautioned with a smile.

"I'm highly adaptable," she told him.

His smile grew broader. "Well then, Tess, what are we waiting for?"

Eleven

Will hadn't been lying to Tess when he'd told her he came up to the roof lot to clear his head. In fact, he'd been coming up here since he was a teenager, when the garage had belonged to his father and the two Darrow men had shared the small apartment beneath the spot where Will was standing now. After his father died, a decade ago, Will hadn't seen any reason to look for a place that was roomier or more conducive to a social life. There were a lot of memories for him here, and he'd just never felt any real reason to move away. He'd found some small solace in continuing to live above the garage and in maintaining what had once been such a daily routine. That routine included coming up to the roof whenever he felt restless or confused.

In the last few weeks Will had been up here a lot. Thinking about Tess. Thinking about his feelings for her. Wondering about her feelings for him. Since the night they had made love, he had been up here nearly every evening, gazing at the sky and thinking. Nursing a beer and thinking. Recalling too many memories to count…and thinking.

And he'd arrived at some interesting conclusions.

First and foremost was his ultimate realization that his feelings for Tess went way beyond a friendly, brotherly concern for his best buddy's kid sister. Yeah, he'd entertained a lot of lascivious—and, as a result, *troubling*—fantasies about her since she'd returned from college, and he'd always chastised himself severely as a result.

And he'd always tried to tell himself that those salacious thoughts resulted from the fact that he was becoming a…a…a lecherous old man. He was pushing forty, after all, and headed right into that decade where men started doing strange stuff to preserve their youth. Strange stuff like, oh…lusting after a sweet young thing ten years their junior, who just so happened to be their best friend's little sister.

At first Will had thought he needed therapy. Now, though, after weeks of thinking, what he realized he needed was Tess.

He wasn't lecherous. He wasn't old. And what he felt for her went way beyond the physical. What he felt for her was love. The kind of love a man feels for a woman he wants to keep by his side forever. He wasn't sure exactly when or how his feelings for her had matured to that point, and he doubted he would ever really know. But his feelings for her had changed. A lot. Just as Tess herself had changed. A lot. And it was those changes in her, he realized, that had brought about the changes in his feelings.

He loved Tess. Deeply. Truly. Eternally. But even figuring that out—finally—had done nothing to help him identify precisely what she felt for him.

Until Finn had said what he had earlier that afternoon, Will had been certain that Tess's feelings for him stemmed from a crush that went back to her childhood. He'd felt so sure that she only cared for him because it had simply become a habit for her, and for no other reason than that. Crushes eventually expired. And even if they didn't expire, they weren't exactly generated by mature, lasting, emotions.

Tess was so young, so inexperienced. Even before Will had realized she was still a virgin, he'd known her sexual knowledge wasn't extensive. She'd never seemed to date many guys and had certainly never had any serious, long-term relationships with anyone. Will had always assumed that the reason for that was because she didn't have serious, long-term feelings for anyone.

Including him.

He'd always thought she just had a crush on him. He'd had no idea she was in love with him. As stupid as it might have seemed to Finn, Will truly had not had an inkling that Tess's feelings were so strong, so adult. But the moment he'd begun to consider it, everything fell into place. It explained why Tess had never dated anyone seriously. It explained why she had never seemed to have strong feelings for anyone.

It explained why she had been a virgin when he'd made love to her that first time.

She loved him. It all made sense now. And how fortunate, how incredibly lucky he was. Because he loved Tess, too. His feelings, too, made sense to him now.

And now, as he gave her a hand up from the stairs and tugged her gently through the hole in the roof, he felt as if the two of them were walking into the sunlight after years of being in the dark. Which was ironic, because the sun had nearly set over the landscape of Marigold, leaving a few streaks of red and orange and pink and lavender in its wake. It was a spectacular sunset. Just perfect for the occasion.

"Wow," Tess said, turning in a slow rotation to take in the complete panorama. "This is amazing. I wouldn't have thought it would make such a difference to come up here, but it does."

"Yeah, it's nice," Will agreed. But he wasn't looking at the scenery. He was looking at Tess. "It kind of leaves you with no other choice but to think about things."

She nodded. "I can see that, definitely."

She turned to gaze at him, and he realized she was blushing. But he couldn't tell if that was because she was thinking about the last night the two of them had spent together or about this one.

"Tess, I—"

"Will, I—"

They started as one and stopped as one, neither of them seeming to know what to do next. Finally Tess expelled a restless little chuckle that mirrored exactly what Will was feeling himself. Nervous. Happy. Uncertain.

"Ladies first," he said.

But she shook her head. "This is your party. You go first."

He was about to argue with her again, remind her that she was his guest and therefore *she* should be the one to go first, but then he admitted that doing that would just be a lame stall tactic that was bound to lob the ball right back into his court. Tess was right. Coming to the garage roof had been his idea. He just wished he could remember now what he'd had in mind when he'd initially suggested it.

Then he recalled that he hadn't really had anything in mind—nothing in particular, anyway. He'd just wanted to be with Tess, alone, someplace where they could talk and sort things out. Oh, yeah. And he recalled, too, that he had needed for that place to be quiet and secluded, a place where they wouldn't be disturbed. Not just because he wanted to make love to her again—if that was what she wanted, too—but because he wanted to ask her a really important question. *Two* really important questions, in fact. Leading up to them, though, was looking to be a bit tricky.

He inhaled a deep breath before beginning, still not sure what he wanted to say. Then, without even realizing he'd decided to speak, he heard himself blurt out, "Tess, do you love me?"

Okay, so much for question number one.

Her eyes went as round as hubcaps when he completed the query, and her mouth dropped open in shock. "Do I…do I wh-what?" she stammered.

Now Will blew out a breath on a long, ragged sigh. *Good going, Darrow,* he told himself. *Smooth. Very smooth. Nothing like putting a woman on the spot, just when you're hoping she'll spend the rest of her life with you. Man.*

"I'm sorry," he apologized quickly. "That didn't come out right."

Her eyebrows shot up to nearly her hairline. "How else was it supposed to come out?"

"I mean, that didn't come out right, either. Ah, dammit," he muttered. "Tess, someone told me today that you…"

She waited for him to finish the statement, and when he didn't, she spurred him, "That I…?"

Will bit back an impatient sound. "That you...have feelings. For me, I mean."

For a long moment she said nothing, only gazed at him as if he were speaking a language she couldn't understand. And in that long moment Will slowly began to panic. What if Finn was wrong? What if Finn had just been playing a sick joke at Will's expense, to get even with him for deflowering his kid sister? What if Finn was just as misguided as he'd accused Will of being? What if Tess didn't love him at all?

He was about to take his question back, was about to form some idiotic excuse for having uttered it in the first place, when Tess finally, eloquently, replied, "Well, duh."

This time Will was the one to arch his eyebrows. "Duh?" he repeated just as eloquently.

Tess nodded, then switched to shaking her head quickly, as if trying to snap herself out of some drugged stupor. "Yes, duh," she assured him. "I, um, I do have feelings for you, Will, yes. And I'm frankly surprised you didn't know this. Especially since I made it clear in my mom's kitchen four years ago, at my welcome-home party, when I told you what a raging crush I'd always had on you." A pained expression shrank her features. "Unless you've forgotten about that."

Forgotten about that? he echoed to himself. *Forgotten? About that?* How was he supposed to forget about that? About the way she had looked that afternoon, gazing at him with such utter—if somewhat inebriated—trust and adoration, as if she would do *any*thing he said, *any*time he wanted, *any* way he commanded. It had been all he could do that afternoon not to take her by the hand, lead her back to his place and make sweet, satisfying love to her for the rest of the day.

That look, that declaration, had set him on fire. It had also reinforced his conviction that what Tess felt for him was infatuation, not love. And his reaction to that look had been what made Will conclude that he was no better than a dirty old man. How the hell could he forget that afternoon, when it had completely screwed up everything that had happened since?

Man, if only he'd hung around to explore things that afternoon, instead of running off like a coward, he thought now.

"Oh, I remember," he told Tess. "I remember really, really well. I just misunderstood, that was all. I didn't think you…" He halted himself before completing the sentence. "I didn't think," he concluded. "That was all. I didn't realize you were telling me you…loved me."

"I still do, you know," she said softly, bravely, thrusting her chin up a notch, as if daring him to contradict her. "Love you, I mean. I always have loved you." She hesitated only a moment before adding, "I always will."

"Oh, Tess." He expelled a single, humorless chuckle. "I wish…"

"What?"

He shook his head. He wasn't going to start with the *what ifs*. The past was gone. He couldn't get it back. And, hey, he really did have plenty of good memories lingering there. The future, however, was wide open. A clean slate just waiting for new experiences to be jotted down. Tess may not be a part of his past the way she could have been, but she was definitely there, and those memories were definitely sweet. As for Tess in his future…

"I love you, too," he said, seeing no reason to keep that to himself anymore. "Maybe I always have loved you, too, Tess, I don't know. But I do love you now. And I can tell you this with all certainty—I always will love you. Maybe it's taken me a little longer than the average guy to figure things out, but eventually I do figure things out." He smiled. "Like you said, 'Duh.'"

"Oh, Will."

The next thing Will knew, Tess was in his arms, covering his mouth with hers, and he was thinking about how incredibly good it felt to have her there again, wondering how he had survived the past two weeks without her. He roped his arms around her waist and returned her kiss, more fiercely than ever before. She responded by warring with him over possession of the kiss, and he was helpless to stop the smile that uncurled his lips as a result.

"What?" she asked breathlessly, pulling back far enough to look at his face. "What's so funny?"

He shook his head slowly and squeezed her tighter. "Nothing is funny. I just feel so..." He sighed with much satisfaction. "So *good,* Tess. You just make me feel so *good.* And I love you *so much.*"

"You've always had that effect on me," she told him, smiling back. "Ever since I was a kid."

"Yeah, well, lemme tell ya, it took me a while to reconcile that kid business."

Her expression turned serious, resolute. "I'm not a child anymore, Will. I'm a woman."

He met her gaze levelly. "Don't I know it."

She smiled again, her own satisfaction with the situation quite evident. "A woman who loves you very, very much."

He brushed a quick kiss over her temple. "I love you, too. Always."

Their vows uttered, Will bent his head to hers again, brushing his lips lightly across hers once, twice, three times, before slanting his mouth completely over hers for a thorough taste of her. As he deepened the kiss, he

skimmed his hands lower, over the taut swell of her derriere, down along her hips, until he could bunch the fabric
of her dress in his hands. He really, really liked how she
always seemed to wear dresses. Not just because they so
enhanced her beauty, her femininity, but because it made
it so much easier for him to reach those parts of her he
very much wanted to reach.

Darrow, you are one dirty young man, he told himself.
Somehow, though, the realization bothered him not at all.
Because Tess, he knew for a fact, was pretty doggone
brazen herself.

Slowly he lifted her dress higher, up over her knees
and thighs, until he could bunch it around her waist. Then
he splayed his hands open over her bare back, his libido
coming alive at the feel of her warm, silky flesh beneath
his fingertips. Tess tugged his shirttail free of his jeans
and mimicked his gesture, opening her palms over his
naked back. But she soon grew restless and moved her
hands between their bodies, unfastening the buttons of
his shirt one by one.

As she ran her hands over the dark hair on his chest,
Will dipped his hands lower, beneath the soft fabric of
her panties, to explore her just as intimately. Her breath
grew ragged, her actions less focused, as he pushed his
fingers lower still, between her legs, to the damp folds
of skin swollen by her passion.

And then, "Now, Will," she gasped against his neck.
"I want you now. Please. We can do it again later,
slower, but right now I've missed you too much to go
slow."

In response to her demand, he pushed her panties down
until they pooled at her feet, and she readily stepped out
of them, kicking them carelessly away. Then she shoved

his shirt from his shoulders, and he likewise felt the kiss of the early evening summer on his bare skin.

He never had a chance to spread that blanket. He did, however, manage to dance their fiercely entwined bodies over to a glider that had valiantly served him on many a night, as he contemplated life, the universe, and Tess Monahan.

He sat down on the padded cushion and pulled her atop him, so that her legs straddled his thighs. Then he pushed her dress up over her hips, and curved his hands over her naked bottom. For long moments he only kissed her deeply as he softly caressed the satiny skin beneath his fingers. Then, growing impatient, he skimmed one hand up her back and unfastened her bra, filling his greedy palm with her breast.

It was so incredibly erotic, holding Tess's naked flesh without undressing her, their heated bodies exposed beneath the quickly darkening sky. He felt her own hand move down between their bodies again, vaguely noted that her fingers began tugging at the snap of his jeans. Instinctively he arched his hips upward, and she uttered a low, needy sound in response before jerking her own hips against his. She tugged down his zipper, then deftly tucked her hand inside his jeans to free the part of him that strained against his fly.

For long moments she ran her fingers up and down his solid length, rubbing her palm over the taut head until Will thought he would go mad with wanting her. When he didn't think he could tolerate any more, and with one quick, easy gesture, he lifted his hips enough to push down his jeans and free his surging member completely.

Then he pulled Tess down over himself, entering her swiftly, totally. She groaned at the depth of his initial penetration, but there seemed to be none of the pain she'd experienced that first time. He hesitated before continuing, though, allowing her body time to adjust itself to him, allowing the rest of her to realize just how very much he loved her.

"Again," she finally said, the word a mere wisp of breath against his temple.

Will settled his hands on her hips and lifted her higher, then thrust himself upward as he pulled her back down again. After that, Tess took over, rising up on her knees slowly, sliding leisurely back down over him. Again and again she rose and descended, until the friction of their bodies nearly sparked them both to flame. After that Will seized control again, holding her hips firmly in place as he bucked against her, over and over, deeper and deeper.

Within minutes he exploded inside her, his hot essence filling her and hers flowing over him. As if cued by their climax, the fireworks began to go off in Gardencourt Park, shattering in the sky like a kaleidoscopic version of their culmination. The whistle and hiss of one detonation after another rocked the skies as Will and Tess rocked each other. And as those colors slowly faded and fell to the ground, so did the two lovers gradually descend.

But another bright burst followed, and Will took advantage of the brief light to shift their bodies, until he was lying back on the glider with Tess stretched out atop him. For long moments they only lay silently, their bodies still joined, their clothes still in a dreadful state of disarray. Neither of them much cared about that as they watched the play of color and sound as it danced across the night sky.

Then, as a particularly bright burst of color spattered above them, something occurred to Will that didn't surprise him nearly as much as he figured it probably should.

"Tess?" he said softly, curling a strand of her hair loosely around his thumb.

"Hmm?" she asked languidly.

"We, um…we didn't use any protection just now," he said. But instead of causing him grief, the realization only filled him with ironic humor.

"I know we didn't," Tess replied softly, her own voice laced with laughter.

"You, um…you could get pregnant," he pointed out without much alarm.

"Didn't you know?" she murmured. "I'm counting on it." She smiled a dreamy little smile as she turned her face to his. And as another burst of color filled the sky, she asked quietly, "Will, will you marry me?"

And Will smiled a dreamy little smile of his own as he replied, "Sure, Tess. I'd love to."

Epilogue

The bride wore white for her early November wedding, to symbolize her first marriage, her first love, her first of so many things. And if anyone noticed the softly bulging tummy where her waistline used to be—and it went without saying that everyone noticed that—no one offered much in the way of a comment. Except, perhaps, for an occasional knowing smile. Or a playful nudge. Or an expectant look. Or an encouraging nod. Mostly, though, everybody just told Tess that she looked positively radiant.

Now as she and Will toured the reception hall of Our Lady of Lourdes Church, thanking all of their guests for attending the celebration, Tess felt more than radiant. She felt buoyant. She felt triumphant. She felt transcendent. And the thought of going home with Will later, home to the big, Victorian house they had bought from her parents, home where they would bring the next generation of Monahans and Darrows into the world...

Well. Tess just didn't think life could get any better than this.

"Oh, Tess!"

She glanced up at the summons to find Olga Petersen, of the Marigold Craft Circle, teeter-tottering toward her. She carried a large, pastel-colored, cube-shaped package in both arthritic hands, and her smile, as she approached, was, well, knowing.

"The Marigold Craft Circle knitted the baby a complete layette," the elderly woman stated proudly. "Sweater, cap, booties, mittens, blanket, you name it," she added. "We're all just so happy for you and Will, Tessie."

She settled the gift on the table behind Tess, which was bedecked with yellow crepe paper and played host to dozens of other gaily wrapped packages. Whether those gifts were for the wedding, or the baby, though, Tess wouldn't know until she opened them. Something told her, however, that there was an assortment of both.

"Of course, we didn't know if the baby would be a boy or a girl," Mrs. Petersen continued, "so the colors are something of a mix."

"That's so sweet of you, Mrs. Petersen," Tess said. "And Will and I have decided to leave gender a mystery, because we want to be surprised at the delivery." She wanted the rest of Marigold to be surprised, too, which was why no one but she and Will knew that Tess was carrying twins. "Thank you so much." She blushed a bit, then added with a smile, "I have to confess, though, that there was a time when I was afraid the Craft Circle would be knitting my baby a little pair of handcuffs."

Mrs. Petersen gaped in obvious outrage. "Why, Tess.

You can't possibly think that anyone in Marigold actually believed that ridiculous story about you being...you know..."

"Knocked up by the Mob?" Tess supplied helpfully. At least, she thought she was being helpful. Judging by the two bright spots of pink that appeared on Mrs. Petersen's cheeks, however, maybe she could have been a bit less so.

"Um, yes, dear," Mrs. Petersen said quietly. "That's exactly what I was going to say. And I was going to add that no one believed that silly tale. We all knew you weren't that kind of a girl."

"Of course you did," Tess assured the other woman with an indulgent smile.

"Oh, Tess!"

As Mrs. Petersen wandered off, Abigail Torrance and Nancy Rosen stepped up to offer their best wishes, both looking resplendent in bright jewel toned dresses, sapphire for Abigail, emerald for Nancy.

After providing the obligatory chitchat, Nancy piped up, "You know, I knew you and Will were an item all along. It was so obvious."

"We all knew that," Abigail rejoined easily. "Every girl in Marigold knew she didn't have a chance with Will because he's been sweet on you for so long." She met Tess's gaze levelly as she added, "And nobody for a minute believed that you could possibly have anything to do with the Mob. Especially, you know...that."

"Of course not," Tess replied obediently.

"Oh, Tess!"

As Nancy and Abigail strode off to join the buffet line, Tess glanced up to find Susan Gibbs striding toward her, beckoning jovially. In spite of everything, Tess found it impossible to harbor any ill will toward her arch-nemesis and co-worker. After all, if it hadn't been for Susan generating the Mob baby story to begin with, Will Darrow might never have come to his senses and realized how much he loved Tess.

Susan smiled a bit nervously as she paused before Tess, and she looked more than a little anxious, despite the breezy floral dress she wore. She lifted a hand casually to her dark hair and said, "I don't think I've congratulated you yet on landing Will Darrow."

"No, you haven't," Tess agreed with a smile.

But instead of doing so, Susan continued, "Listen, I just want you to know that I never, ever, not even for the tiniest moment, believed that story that was circulating about you last summer."

Tess smiled blandly. "And what story was that, Susan?"

Susan let her gaze stray from Tess's for a moment, then she quickly, if not quite convincingly, recovered her smile. "Oh, never mind," she said. "It was nothing. Just some silly little rumor. You know how the Marigold grapevine works."

"I sure do," Tess said. "But don't worry. That little tidbit I heard from Sister Mary Joseph about you won't go any further than my two lips. I promise. I won't tell a soul, Susan." To illustrate, Tess mimicked the motion of locking her lips with a tiny key, then tossing it over her shoulder.

And as she did, Susan blanched. "What, uh, what little tidbit was that?" she asked quietly.

Tess bit back the mischievous grin she felt threatening. "Oh, it's nothing," she assured the other woman. "I told Sister that it just wasn't possible. That you'd never do something like that with the school funds." She paused a meaningful moment before rushing on, "Or any funds, for that matter. I'm absolutely positive you're not that kind of girl. I mean, honestly. Acapulco? When we need that playground equipment so much more?''

Susan grinned, albeit a bit anxiously. Then, "Um, thanks, Tess, for not spreading rumors,'' she murmured. But she didn't sound any too comfortable when she said it. And Tess offered nothing more by way of an explanation. Surely Susan knew she was only kidding.

Surely.

"Oh, Tess!''

She was about to growl impatiently under her breath at yet another local citizen reassuring her that no one had ever believed, not even for a minute, that silly tale that everyone had believed, for a lot longer than a minute, when she glanced up this time to see Will sauntering toward her. Will. Her husband. The father of her children. Now that was a story whose time had finally come.

She thought he looked so handsome in his pearl gray morning coat and trousers, but he was clearly uncomfortable in such attire. Now that the wedding ceremony was over and the reception was winding down, he was tugging impatiently at his ascot, and she noticed he'd already unbuttoned his vest. But even in a state of disarray, he was still the most breathtaking man she'd ever known.

"When can we leave?'' he asked without preamble once he stood close enough that no one would be able to hear.

"What?'' she asked, feigning surprise. "Don't tell me you're not having a good time.''

"Oh, I'm having a good time,'' he assured her. "In between all our guests telling me they never believed for a moment that you were knocked up by the Mob.'' He shook his head slowly, as if he couldn't believe the shallowness of some people. "I don't know why they couldn't see through that stupid story as quickly as I did."

She smiled. "It is a mystery," she agreed.

But Tess didn't hold anyone's reaction against them, because she knew the people of Marigold always saw the best in a situation. She also knew they had very short memories when it came to making mistakes. She knew they'd only seen the truth about the Mob baby after Finn had pointed out to everyone what was really going on with Tess—and Will. But she didn't think any less of her neighbors. That was the way small towns worked. And besides, whatever had happened in the past, well, it was the past. And as much as she would cherish many of those memories, Tess was much more content to envision the years ahead.

"So...can we go home now?" Will asked again, very hopefully this time.

She nodded. "I don't think anyone would hold it against us."

He grinned cockily as he pulled her into his arms. "Good. 'Cause I want to hold you against me. All night long."

"Mmm," she murmured as she settled her cheek against his chest. "Sounds like a great way to start our honeymoon."

She felt his soft sigh of contentment and smiled.

"You sure you don't want to go to the Virgin Islands or something instead?" he asked.

She laughed. "No," she told him. "For some reason, they just don't hold the appeal one might think. I like what we have planned much better."

"Okay," he said. "If you're sure you want me to go ahead and paint that other room..."

She nodded. "And then I want you to paint all the other ones, too. Something tells me we're going to be using them all. Eventually."

Will smiled down at Tess as she gazed back up at him. "Then what are we waiting for?" he asked.

She smiled back. "Not a thing, Will. Not a thing."

*   *   *   *   *

Silhouette®

where love comes alive—online...

eHARLEQUIN.com

your romantic escapes

—Indulgences—

♥ Monthly guides to indulging yourself,
such as:
★ Tub Time: A guide for bathing beauties
★ Magic Massages: A treat for tired feet

—Horoscopes—

♥ Find your daily Passionscope, weekly
Lovescopes and Erotiscopes

♥ Try our compatibility game

—Reel Love—

♥ Read all the latest romantic
movie reviews

—Royal Romance—

♥ Get the latest scoop on your favorite
royal romances

—Romantic Travel—

♥ For the most romantic destinations, hotels
and travel activities

SINTE1

You're not going to believe this offer!

In October and November 2000, buy any two Harlequin or Silhouette books and save $10.00 off future purchases, or buy any three and save $20.00 off future purchases!

Just fill out this form and attach 2 proofs of purchase (cash register receipts) from October and November 2000 books and Harlequin will send you a coupon booklet worth a total savings of $10.00 off future purchases of Harlequin and Silhouette books in 2001. Send us 3 proofs of purchase and we will send you a coupon booklet worth a total savings of $20.00 off future purchases.

Saving money has never been this easy.

I accept your offer! Please send me a coupon booklet:

Name: _____

Address: _____ City: _____

State/Prov.: _____ Zip/Postal Code: _____

Please send this form, along with your cash register receipts as proofs of purchase, to:
In the U.S.: Harlequin Books, P.O. Box 9057, Buffalo, NY 14269
In Canada: Harlequin Books, P.O. Box 622, Fort Erie, Ontario L2A 5X3
(Allow 4-6 weeks for delivery) Offer expires December 31, 2000.   PHQ4002

COMING NEXT MONTH

CMN1000